PRAISE FOR KRISTOPHER TRIANA

"Triana has a voice unmatched by other writers in his field. His short stories pack more punch than your average novel. Beware of this man's words, for they are dangerous and contagious."
　　　—Max Booth III, author of *Toxicity*

"Triana's work really brings the thunder!"
　　　—Jon Mikl Thor, musician, bodybuilder and actor
　　　(*Rock N' Roll Nightmare, Zombie Nightmare*)

"Kristopher Triana's short story collection is a great read. His stories will keep you engaged and I have to say I am not easily frightened, but I caught myself white-knuckling a few times. Thanks for the ride, Kris!"
　　　—Liane Curtis, actress
　　　(*Sixteen Candles, Critters 2, Sons of Anarchy*)

"Triana's writing will make your soul feel like more maggots are raining out of it than in a Fulci film. It's hyper reality crossed with the monsters under your bed — and they're going to fight for your fear."
　　　—Eric Martin, *Guts and Grog*

MORE PRAISE FOR KRISTOPHER TRIANA

GROWING DARK

by

Kristopher Triana

A Blue Juice Publication - Palm Bay, FL

Published by Blue Juice, a division of Blue Juice Films, Inc.
730 Campina Ave., Palm Bay, FL 32909

Editor - Thomas Mumme
Copy Editor - Megan Miller
Layout Editor - Adam Miller

Cover Art - Michael Crockett
Cover Design - Adam Miller
Crow Illustration - Cora Triana

"From the Storms, A Daughter" was originally published in *Earth's End*, an anthology by Wicked East Press (2010)

"Video Express" was originally published in *The Ghost is the Machine*, an anthology by Post Mortem Press (2012)

"Giving from the Bottom" was originally published in *Spinetingler Magazine* (October 2011 issue)

"Legends" was originally published in *Zombie Jesus and Other True Stories*, an anthology by Dark Moon Books (2012)

"The Bone Orchard" was originally published in *How the West Was Wicked*, an anthology by Pill Hill Press (2011)

"Before the Boogeymen Come" was originally published in *Wretched Moments*, an anthology by Pill Hill Press (2010)

Library of Congress Control Number: 2015933758
ISBN - 978-1-940967-96-7
FIRST PRINTING.

for Cora
my everything

ACKNOWLEDGEMENTS

This book would not have been possible without the help, dedication, vision and lifelong friendship of Thomas Mumme, the best buddy a writer could have. Special thanks also goes to everyone at Blue Juice for believing in this project and putting so much effort into it. Thanks to Megan Miller for her editing skills and completing the difficult task of cleaning up my errors and occasional made-up words. Appreciation to the good folks at *Post Mortem Press, Spinetingler Magazine, Dark Moon Books, Pill Hill Press,* and *Wicked East Press* for publishing some of these stories the first time around and for giving exposure to independent authors everywhere. Thanks also to my dog Bear for always being by my side as I type feverishly into the night.

TABLE OF CONTENTS

From the Storms, A Daughter

The rain was black.

It fell upon the sullen landscape, just as it had for weeks now without ceasing — a fluid curtain of despair. Even daylight hours turned dusk-like now as it slammed down, its ferocity merciless. The storms refused to weaken or give the flood's survivors even a moment of hope to breathe — the human survivors, anyway, for there were always *the others*.

Lee thought about them now as he sped through the murk that used to be Main Street. *Those others* — the myths that had become popular conversation pieces inside the shelters. *Just the crazy talk of the devastated*, he told himself, the very sorts of delusions he'd seen in countless people who'd been stricken by the paralyzing backhand of sudden grief, including himself.

He pushed away the morbid image of Helen that flickered into his mind.

The rain had been bad from the start when, weeks ago, the clouds had formed over the Cape and had begun to churn like a witch's cauldron. It had come forth like a squall, so fierce and unexpected that it was fascinating until it instilled panic. But it wasn't until a few days later that the rain began to grow darker, and then became pitch black. It was inklike now. It was still water, not oil or sludge, but tainted rain pouring down into a ghost land.

The small New England town of Waltower had been flooded for several weeks. As usual, basements were the first to go, then businesses and homes. The drainage systems had eventually backed up, and the flood had merged with the raw sewage in a sickening synergy. Emergency response from Washington had been slow and pathetic, and all public servants, including beat cops like Lee, had been working long hours without days off. It was grueling at first, but at this point Lee was past the stress of overworking. Even the terror concerning the children failed to sink into Lee any longer.

He wasn't exactly numb; he was just used to the suffering now, jaded. He'd been a cop for almost five years, and that was all the time his mind had needed to be pounded into a pit of negativity. Forty-five hours a week spent with the most damaged forms of human life; how many dead bodies had he seen, long before this black flood that offered many random, bloated floaters? How many nights had he sprung upward in bed to be comforted by Helen's groggy embrace as he still shivered from the reflections of his workday? How many mornings had he searched through his family Bible for answers he could not decipher?

The portable police scanner buzzed with a static-filled voice, bringing Lee back from his cyclonic thoughts. He slowed the boat, and a fragment of the sign from Sabuccili's Pizzeria clunked against the side before drifting on past the fat carcass of a dog as it, too, bobbed on the water, carrying maggots like a dinghy of death.

The receiver hissed with the crackling sound of Sergeant Harkman's strained voice.

"Calling all scouting units ..."

"10-4, Sergeant," Lee replied.

Lee heard a few other scouting units reply as well, including Taidem, Monroe, Rodriguez, and Lee's partner, Sarah Cohen.

Harkman was to the point: "We've got more refugees from outside of Massachusetts coming in to use our shelters. We're gonna need some of you back for escorting duties."

Pulling the others in, Harkman advised Lee and Sarah to remain on scouting patrol and to meet one another at Union Square, thereby giving each of them equal ground to cover before meeting back at the center of town. Lee could sense the apprehension in Harkman's voice. He didn't take it too personally. It was just pity, which Lee didn't want or need from anyone anymore.

A sudden thud brought him out of his thoughts. It was a quick thump that rocked the boat to the left, followed by splashing, like small limbs flailing in the water. He scooted over to the other side of the craft and peered into the rippling blackness below. He saw his own timeworn reflection in it, appearing far beyond his 34 years, his brow sunken above the two shaded caves of his eyes. At first he thought he saw a slimy tree branch spin up to the surface, but then the branch arched itself like the back of a mad wolf, and wheeled forward.

This ain't no branch.

He wondered if it was some sort of fish that had washed in from the overflow of the river, but he could not make out any features. It was more like a slick, purplish, overgrown worm that churned, its off-black coat glimmering like a string of rubies. Before Lee could react, the thing had returned to the water, sinking, only to be followed by another. This one rose higher out of the water than its sibling had, its pointed tip flailing; the small, circular suckers of its underbelly feeling the damp air. These were not worms, or even snakes, Lee realized; they were tentacles, all belonging to one creature.

Lee spun at the waist and grabbed for his floodlight as the second tentacle returned to the abyss of Main Street, descending. At first the light just shined on the surface of the water, but as his eyes adjusted, he could see debris sailing deep within the sludge: a rusted bicycle wheel, a flannel shirt, a headless Barbie doll. Then, suddenly, there was the smooth back of a swimming thing whose bulk had a triangular form, like a stingray. The sinew pulsated within its unconventional frame, looking like misshapen spheres rolling underneath its scales. One tentacle reached out in each direction, like a compass made of gelatin. Lee stared at the beast for a few moments before it sunk away, its final trace being but a few bubbles that rose, popped, and emitted a sour marsh gas. He stood up and shot the beam all around the water where the thing had lurked, but the creature had lost him, having vanished into underwater shadows.

The rain grew blacker.

* * * * *

Less than three miles away, Sarah drew her own motorboat closer to the ruins of the library. The building was now a shell of itself, its pillars slathered in algae. Its windows, shattered from looters, looked like the jagged mouths of jack-o-lanterns, while the front doors had broken off and long since floated away.

"Hello?" Sarah called out again, her echo bouncing back at her. She couldn't see much through the doorway. It was submerged to a third of the way up. The water had leveled the area, and now she could coast right up — that is, if she really wanted to. There was something not right about what she had seen, something foreboding, and the silence that replied to her every time she called out caused her even more concern.

She had to get people out of the town, whether they liked it or not. It wasn't just a rescue mission anymore; it was the enforcement of the mandatory evacuations. She'd been through a few natural disasters before, and she knew from experience that there were always those stubborn folks who refused to abandon their homes and the town they'd always lived in.

"Hello in there?" she called out again. *Damn it, not another hide-and-seeker.*

She knew she wasn't seeing things, even if the rain was capable of creating illusions from the dim light. She knew that as she had come closer to the library, she'd heard a distinct splashing, like feet stomping through the water. She'd directed her floodlight at the opening in the building, and a short, white, human form had ducked for cover when the light had hit it. She'd seen only a twitch of pale skin as the body sloshed away behind the walls, looking like a filthy porcelain doll skipping about in a frenzy. Then there was darkness, with only silence as a companion.

"There's a mandatory evacuation!" she said. "You need to come out now!"

She'd called out to this person several times now. She was no longer trying to coax them out, she was ordering them. Still she received no reply. She shone the light into the doorway, but a few feet away. She could see that the library offered only slight shelter, its roof leaking in many places. Her light revealed the flooded lobby: the bowed bookshelves, tilted and submerged, some of the paperbacks sailing about.

The boat was too wide to make it through the entrance. Though it was a two-door entryway, there was a strong divider in the middle. She hated the idea of getting out of the boat and stepping into contaminated water, but Sarah knew that this, too, was part of her job, and she wasn't about to abandon her code now. She would just have to hope that her galoshes and her fisherman slacks would be a secure enough shield. Balancing herself with her flashlight in hand, she maneuvered over the side of the boat and onto something that wasn't as sturdy. It was soft and malleable, and as she moved, it moved too, spinning beneath her. She fell backward, the blob pushing out from under her. She braced herself against the boat, and her skin went gooseflesh as the thing she'd stepped on rose to the surface. Her free hand reached for her shoulder holster. She brought her pistol out just as the gray mass reached the surface of the water.

Sarah knew, as soon as she could see it, that it wasn't alive. Directing her light on it, she could make out the many sores that covered it, wounds so fresh that they still trickled brightly with blood. Poking at the mass with her pistol, she managed to get it to spin, flipping it over.

She realized then that it was a human torso.

Horror pounced upon her, her heart hammering. For this wasn't merely another sad floater like all of the others she'd had the misfortune of raking in. No, this man had been savagely ripped to pieces. The flood could have drowned him, but something must have severed his limbs, decapitated him, and eviscerated him so that half of his intestines spilled outward. It was not an old corpse either, for she quickly ascertained that the decomposition was meager. Only bloating had begun on the pruned flesh, the man's skin having turned grayer with death.

Suddenly she wondered what had been holding it down beneath the water.

Sarah climbed back into the boat so hastily that she dropped her flashlight and the motorboat rocked as she fell back into it. She peered over the edge, looking down at her flashlight as it sank. It spiraled as it descended, its beam illuminating the mysterious murk, revealing a galaxy of churning index cards and pencils, as well as a gray severed hand and some disconcerting sinew from an unrecognizable piece of the carcass. But as the beam circled the library, something else came into view.

"Oh, dear God," she whispered.

The face Sarah saw deep within the water bore a complexion white as polished ivory, intensifying the inhuman blankness of its expression. She could see thin strands obscuring the features, either hair or seaweed or more sinew upon its bulbous head, hanging down before its eyes. The eyes were all pupils; expressionless, black orbs like a shark's, too far apart and not exactly level with one another. As the light fell further, Sarah could see that this face bore no nose, only nostrils. Beneath this, a mouth was chewing, the lower jaw propelling its jagged teeth, tearing more flesh away from the mangled leg of the carcass. Then the beam of light fell further downward, spinning to the right of this piscine thing that lunched upon the dead man's pieces below.

The terror Sarah felt upon seeing this, though all-encompassing, was not quite as disturbing as the fact that it had triggered her memory. Though not identical to that of the monstrosity below, there was another face she knew of that was eerily similar. Though the two faces were not one and the same, she understood immediately that there was a connection, one that made Sarah's blood run cold.

"Beth," she whimpered.

She thought of some of the snippets of conversation she'd heard in the shelters, the stories that were told each night. She'd dismissed it as mass hallucination, even after what had happened to her partner, Lee, and his poor wife, Helen. Even now, as she struggled to start the motor, she didn't want to believe any of it. The madness of it first outweighing the horror of it, then the horror of it germinating within her until her entire body began to shudder like an open gate in an aimless October wind. On the third pull, the motor came alive and, just as the water beneath it started to foam, a wave splashed toward her. The creature, startled by the motor, erupted from the corner, its wiry arms flailing as its misshapen head shook, its hair whipping in the dank. It shrieked like a tortured raccoon.

With a scream of her own, Sarah began shooting, and as the flash of the gunfire created a strobe light in the catacombs of the library, she could see that the upper body of this thing she was now firing upon resembled that of a young boy.

* * * * *

Lee wondered now if the legends could be true. He knew he was caving in to the notion just by thinking of them as legends rather than as mad nonsense: the tales of family tragedies in which missing children had been found as twisted versions of their previous selves.

The missing children, Lee despaired to think, *so many of them*.

This was the primary objective of the scouting missions. Most citizens were accounted for, but there was an alarming number of missing children in the county, many of whom had mysteriously wandered away from the shelters and had never returned. There was enough curious dread afflicting the suffering survivors already, with the flooding and the sudden, drastic increase in pregnancies. The walls of the shelter were lined with women whose stomachs were swollen. It was almost too horrible to bear, this terribly real threat of losing more innocent children to the flood, especially some who remained unborn.

Lee sighed, tears brewing as his face pinched. The word came out of him in a murmur, the soft tone one uses to talk only to oneself as one cries alone.

"Beth," he whispered. "Oh, Beth."

* * * *

The radio was worthless now. She wasn't sure if she was being heard, but she'd requested immediate assistance, and had given specifics as to where she was traveling. Terror pulsed through her, the sickening thrum of fear permeating her consciousness with the severity of a wound.

The ghoulish creature that had wallowed in the library had looked just as Lee had described Beth. The realization of this was chilling, but not as chilling as the suggestions her mind began to offer up to her.

Dear God, could it all be true?

She was worried for Lee now, even more than she had been in the past few weeks, which was a great deal.

Sarah remembered how good-natured he had been during those first few days on the force. Lee was one of those rare individuals who joined the police department with the earnest intention of making the world a better place for everyone. He also expressed a sense of camaraderie with the entire station, throwing smiles and back pats to every cop he came across. This friendliness, like all kindness, was immediately mistaken for weakness, and Lee was subsequently bullied and emotionally hazed by his jaded colleagues.

While working the beat, she'd watched the outside world and the job it created for them transform Lee. Instead of finding himself a beloved local pillar, he instead found himself to be little more than a referee in the vicious game of human interaction.

Sarah had been forced to watch him morph into another sad, quiet hulk of a man who armored himself with a slack expression and hid behind lifeless eyes. There was still an enormous amount of compassion buried within Lee, but he refused to share it with the world any longer. But he was always friendly with her, more so than any other cop she'd worked with, and he was a dedicated partner. He was this way with her because, unlike most people, she'd never given him reason not to be. But it was not merely their own interaction as partners that assured her that the warmhearted Lee still existed somewhere deep inside the hollowed hull of his social self: She had seen the way he was with his wife.

Sarah had been over to Lee and Helen's home several times for barbecues and holiday gatherings. Lee's behavior around his wife was tenfold what his early behavior as a rookie cop had been. Watching the two of them together was like watching two teenagers in the midst of a summer fling, wandering on the fading edge of a starry night. They had been married for two years and together for five, and they were still giddy lovers and not ashamed to show it.

When news arrived that Lee and Helen would soon be starting a family, something cracked open within Lee's coarse external shell, and Lee relapsed and reverted to his former, good-natured self.

Helen was eight and a half months pregnant when the rains came.

Like so many other expectant mothers, she had ended up making her delivery in the makeshift maternity ward at the shelter, with Lee at her side behind the strung white sheets. The humid night had been hideously black, the stars blotted out. The delivery itself had been brutal: an extended labor that tortured poor Helen and brought her to the brink of madness before releasing her into a dangerous coma. The medical staff had struggled to save the unborn infant, who had been trying to come out backward, by performing an emergency cesarean section. Lee had refused to leave his wife's side, even as they'd sliced open her swollen belly.

But his baby daughter had been stillborn. Her body still looked fetal, coiled around itself in a sad huddle. Her oddly open eyes were fully black, and her wide mouth had not yet formed lips, but had somehow begun growing imperfect, jagged teeth. When he'd looked closer at her tiny corpse, he was mortified by what he'd found. A thin wire of flesh was encircled around her throat, causing her to be strangled during her birth. Lee had thought at first, just as the medial staff had, that his daughter had been choked by the umbilical cord, but this was not so. Upon closer inspection, they could make out the umbilical cord beneath a thick veil of plasma, winding from the infant's belly up into Helen's insides. The thin wire of flesh that was wrapped around the baby was connected to her but not to the mother. It was an auxiliary limb that grew out of the small of the infant's back. It was the strange, fleshy growth of a mutant, a birth defect that resembled something closer to the anatomy of a small squid than that of a human being.

The medical staff had tried valiantly to save Helen's life, and failed, just as they had failed to bring Beth into the world. Sarah had watched Lee disintegrate since the tragedy, which was really only one of many such tragedies. But Sarah knew now that something more troublesome was unfurling itself across this suffering little New England town: a bizarre horror that was metamorphosing within the buried city and deep within the wombs of its mothers. Sarah sped on, like a lost child, her consciousness stunned

by the terror that had been cast over her like the shadow of
the rain itself.

* * * * *

Lee first noticed her as she squatted upon the half-
submerged pile of concrete. She was merely a toddler,
nude, wet, and a soft shade of gray. She was hunched over,
her green hair obscuring the thing in her hands. He was
fascinated by the rubbery jiggling of her limbs, her arms
working like snakes, looking boneless as they twisted with
her feeding. As the boat drifted closer, she looked up,
noticing him, her eyes freezing upon him even as her
puppet-like mouth flapped, still gnawing the strip of meàt.
He looked closer.
She was feasting on the innards of a dead cat.
While the sight would revolt most, Lee was instead
overcome by a quick brainstorm, linking the pieces of a
macabre puzzle. He marveled now at the sudden notion:
reverse evolution. The thought hit him with the force of a
sledgehammer. *It's Darwinism gone berserk*, he thought.
Still, it began to not only make sense, but he could almost
fathom a biblical providence to it all.
Perhaps, Lee thought, God or nature or whatever it
may be had grown weary of the brutality of humankind.
Some immaculate force had gazed too long upon the cruel
anarchy that humans had made for themselves. Perhaps this
divine entity shared Lee's disappointment in humankind,
and had now initiated not just an extinction, but a
transformation in which human beings reverted back to sea
creatures, and rapidly relapsed into an aquatic state of cold-

blooded solipsism, as if God was starting again from scratch.

In this girl with a face like a piranha, Lee saw not a monster, but the first baby of a new world, like a mutated Christ child who had passed through some fathomless membrane to become the new link in biology. And while Lee had previously been considering himself to be like Job, now he could see himself as Noah, sailing through God's merciless downpour as a rescuer of his creatures.

He brought the boat closer to the girl, who continued to stare him down as she gnashed her feline tripe. With the motor dead, the only sound was of the rain colliding with the endless pool.

"Hello, sweet pea," he said with a warm smile.

She stared blankly. He made attempts at friendliness, as he tended to do with all children. He winked and waved, crouching a little to see her better behind her cloak of rot-colored hair.

"You remind me a lot of my little girl," he said, smiling, hoping to spark her interest. She only belched, her giant mouth spitting gray bits.

Lee smiled wider as he cried, his heart swelling while his mind fragmented. He turned around, reaching for the surplus cooler. He took a large strip of jerky and held it out to her. He watched as the gills twinkled, expanding at the promise of flesh. She let the cat plop and began crawling toward the boat, watching him nervously.

"It's OK," he told her.

He placed the jerky a foot away from himself, hoping she would be brave enough to come aboard. The maneuver worked, and he was pleased to see her writhe onto the craft.

She chomped down on the jerky ravenously. During this feeding frenzy, she occasionally bellowed with delight, obviously enjoying the snack. The sound she omitted was far from human: a curious bleating, like that of a dolphin struggling against a net.

Both of them flinched at the rising sound of a motor whirring closer to them. Its steady approach made the newfound girl nervous, and Lee calmed her with more jerky and a continuation of his comforting words, assuring her with soft nothings.

* * * * *

The sight of the two of them together made Sarah shudder. She pushed her coat away from her holster as she pulled up to them, wary of the child.

"Lee?" she called out to him over the sounds of the storm.

He was silent for a moment, as if hypnotized by the foul thing that crouched beside him now, feasting.

"Lee? What is going on?"

"Isn't it incredible, Sarah?"

"Get away from it, Lee. It's dangerous."

He was deaf to her words.

"It's like some kind of miracle," he said. "After all this suffering, all this sacrifice, finally there's a light."

"Lee, listen to me ..."

"From all this darkness," he began, "came all of this confusion and misery. But there was a purpose all along, a painful but necessary change, you see? The changes took my little daughter, and gave us these storms ... and from the storms, a daughter."

With these words, he gestured to the creature beside him with his open palms, as if presenting this ghastly thing as a blessing.

"Lee," she cried, "this isn't your daughter! She isn't human! Something's gone wrong in this town Lee, something's taking over."

Sarah lunged from her own boat into Lee's, grabbing his arm. But her sudden movements startled the girl, and she sprang upward in a fit of violence, clawing at Sarah's legs. Her talons spun as they sawed into her. As her blood spattered into the face of the screeching girl, Sarah drew her pistol. She screamed just before the crack of the gunshot echoed throughout the doomed little town.

* * * * *

Lee placed his still-smoking pistol down on the cooler, waiting for the boat to steady itself from the impact of Sarah's fallen body. His shot had been straight to her skull, ending her life as mercifully as he could, under the conditions. She'd fallen, landing half in his boat and half in her own, rocking both of them but tipping neither.

The girl was still rattled, but it was nothing a little jerky and lullabies couldn't fix. She bleated quietly now as he cooed at her, coaxing her back to him. She perched on the end of the boat like a gargoyle, her webbed feet gripping the base so hard that it began to crack.

"Don't worry, baby," he said. "Daddy took care of things. She can't hurt you now. I won't let anybody hurt you, I promise."

She was beginning to calm down, he could see that, but still she seemed more interested in Sarah's remains than in him or even the jerky strip. She stared at Sarah with those oversized eyes of pure black, like two eight balls hammered into the face of a doll.

After a moment, Lee nodded at her, understanding. He reached across the gap between the boats and lifted Sarah, dragging her carcass entirely into his boat. He placed her shattered head at the front, directly below the girl, who still hovered like a vulture. This helping was fresh, not like the cat had been. Lee sat back and let her enjoy the full serving he had provided for her. He'd lost everything he held dear, but now he had something to hold on to, someone to protect once again. He watched as she dug into Sarah's brains, feasting in a more gluttonous display than before.

"Enjoy, sweet pea," he told her. "Everything's going to be just fine. I'll always protect you, and I'll make sure there's *always plenty of food*."

Tears burned in the corners of his eyes as she looked up from the carnage of her meal. She bleated happily in a mist of blood.

"I love you too, Beth," he replied.

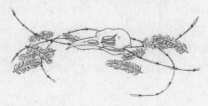

Eaters

We'd only been out there for 10 days when I began to start thinking about eating Bill. All of Osceola County had gone mean and dry, but the ruins of Yeehaw Junction was the most destitute. It'd grown to mirror some of the nearby ghost towns since the disease had spread. There was an eerie, desolate quality to the streets, and the mangled houses seemed to melt there under the vicious Florida sun. It was summer, there hadn't been any rain, and the air stank from the brushfires caused by the drought and chaos.

There were four of us patrolling 18 blocks, one of many units put together at City Hall in the wake of the outbreak. Ed was the lawman, a middle-aged deputy with an inflamed nose to match his stocky build. Then there was David, the college boy down from FSU, with his spongy, long hair and his clever T-shirts. He'd been going for a medical degree before the disaster hit, so he served as our makeshift medic, the pros being far too busy with the overcrowded hospitals. I was just a Good Samaritan, and I'll have you know that I volunteered for survivor patrol before they instituted that new draft. Before trying to become a preacher, I'd worked as a ranch hand. I'm good with my mitts, having spent most of my life cropping hay and such. More importantly, I'm good with animals. Calving, branding, tagging, roping, slaughtering — you name it, I've done it. I reckon this is what got that Army recruiter so excited about me in the first place, 'cause what we were dealing with out there was more *animal* than anything else.

But I guess I should get back to Bill.

He was a cafeteria worker at the high school in St. Cloud, the nearest one to Yeehaw, which had had a small population even before the disease ravaged the place. Bill was older than me, in his late 40s, tall and thin if you ignored his beer belly. He smoked a lot, and his teeth were crooked and as yellow as custard. He also liked to lope. Hell, more than that, the man was just plain lazy. His dragging ankles held up our searches most of the time, and Ed gave him grief about it a lot, being our troop leader and all. Bill was one of the drafted who really resented being drafted in the first place, and so he chose to make his bad situation worse by moping all the time like a whore for pity. The kid, David, had been drafted too, but he was fast, smart, and useful. He didn't piss and moan like Bill, and he also had an admirable sense of patriotic duty, which I'd always thought was lacking in his generation. David had been pulled in, but he was proud and happy to help. But not ol' Bill. Oh no. He was limp weight. That's why we mostly just made him carry our extra stuff.

People might think I targeted Bill for devouring first because he was the weakest team member. That would make sense, but that wasn't it. He also wasn't appealing physically — as meat chops, I mean. David was the youngest and had the least amount of hair and fat on him. He would have been the cleanest and leanest selection. Ed was the most muscular — a lot of steaks to be had there. Bill, however, looked like he'd just stumbled out of rehab, like he was carrying unusual STDs and simply wasn't big on soap.

But when that special kind of hunger hits, there ain't no rational thinking like that involved. It's a chemical thing, a need. An alcoholic doesn't slam back a bottle of Jack because he's thirsty. He doesn't even do it because he wants to get sauced. He does it out of sheer physical need. That is what the hunger is like. I didn't choose Bill, the hunger did. I was just a tool of the plague, even if I had been in denial of it ever since I'd found the little girl.

* * * * *

The patrol unit's main job was survivor recovery. With that job came the other jobs of test administration, tagging and reporting for transfer, and flat-out zombie killing. The real danger zones were infiltrated by the military — you know, all those places that were beyond hope and just swarming with the flesh-eating bastards. These zones were designated as such and were eliminated by bullets and flame. Most of your major metropolitan areas had met this fate. Overpopulated cities like Orlando had been too good a breeding ground for the plague, and it had spread like butter over a hot Christmas goose. There was nothing to do but eliminate the problem before it could spread beyond its borders. Survivors were, unfortunately, just considered casualties of war when those flame-throwers came out.

But these here small towns, tucked in between east of nowhere and west of jack-squat, these were considered unmarked zones. Patrol units like ours would sort of survey the area. We'd call in for rescue buses when we'd gathered survivors, shoot any full-fledged zombies we came across, and give the serum tests to any questionable cases. By doing this, we could evaluate what the zone needed next. If more firepower was needed to destroy a warehouse full of raving ghouls, we could request that assistance. If the area was mostly clean, we could start a safer evacuation. We were kind of like the census of a post-zombie-apocalyptic world. But the most vital part of our mission, beyond killing zombies and even rescuing survivors, was tracking the disease itself.

A lot of people still don't realize that this zombie plague ain't always fatal. Z1V1, as the scientists call it, is like any other virus. Some people with weak immune systems, like old folks or the sickly, they succumb to it almost instantly. David told me that their cells just aren't strong enough to fight it off. But some people have strong enough immune systems to kick the virus after a few days. They'd get a bad flu, their skin would get that grayish-green zombie hue, and they'd start acting funny, sniffing other people like they were a bag of ground coffee and such. But after a few days or sometimes a week, they could fully recover. They would not become a member of the walking dead; they would just teeter there on the threshold for a spell in a sort of zombie limbo. But then they would come out of it restored to normal and even immune to the virus for good. The only problem was that sometimes in that interval, the virus would be going real strong like, and it would rattle their thinking too much. The inner itch of the zombie would take charge, and, well, they'd up and eat somebody.

It's not quite as easy for people to turn back around after a thing like that. They still don't become zombies, but mentally and emotionally, most folks collapse. Cannibalism can do that to you. It's the perfect precursor to a nervous breakdown. A damn good share of the survivors we found were perfectly healthy physically, but fell into a comatose state when they came out of their zombie fever and found that they'd eaten their kids. We found a lot of these types of survivors huddled in their attics or closets, just shaking, crying, and raving, many still caked with the blood of their loved ones.

We called them the part-time cannibals. I reckon it was not the most sensitive term, but, as any war vet will tell you, only humor can get you through living in hell. These part-time cannibals could be rehabilitated, of course, if they weren't too far gone. We would tag them for therapy and ship them out on the buses when they came to round them up. But some of them had such a case of the crazies that it was hard to tell them apart from the zombies. Others were still in the first stages of the virus, too, and you couldn't be sure if they were going to recover.

That was where the serum test came into play.

It was simple. David called it "holistic." The serum was made almost entirely of clean human plasma. Each batch was separated into vials, similar to individual doses of eyedrops that you'd break off of plastic strips. In the human body, Z1V1 takes time to spread. But a small portion of clean tissue can show infection instantly and violently. A few drops of blood from a hopelessly infected person would go gray, curdle like a hot bucket of old cream, and then start popping and spraying inside the tube as it just grew greener and greener. That was when you knew you had a terminal case and you had to pop a round into the back of the poor bastard's skull. But if the serum didn't have a reaction, it meant that the cells in the person's blood were conquering the virus and that they'd be clean in a few days, and would be mentally sound, as long as you could keep them from gnawing off your face in the interval. Which brings me to the difficult part of all of this: drawing the blood from the zombies and part-time cannibals. I would hold my rifle steady on them. Ed would pop them with the taser. Bill would pin down their necks, usually with a chair or broom, so they couldn't bite if they regained their motor skills too quickly. But David was quick. He would run in there with the syringe and get their blood before they could move again, and then we could run the test. Depending on the outcome, I'd either put my rifle away, or I'd put it to use.

* * * * *

We'd been scouting Yeehaw for a week when it happened.

The old hick town was nearly deserted, and the lack of action had made us all too bored and relaxed. We'd spent the day searching one empty house after another. No zombies, no part-timers, no living people; just dead bodies. It was just the four of us and a tree line full of well-fed buzzards. Most of us had started to feel like we were wasting our time and that we should just declare the zone vacant. But Ed was a by-the-book cop, an old-fashioned kind of dude who took his job seriously. There wasn't a shower curtain in town he wasn't going to pull back, not a car trunk he wasn't going to pry open. He was going to have us peer into every crevice in Yeehaw before he'd ever file a damn report.

"Anything in the master bedroom?" Ed asked David as he came back from it. We were searching through the last house on a dead-end road. It was one story, but it seemed to go on forever.

"Nothing of interest."

Ed turned to Bill.

"Find anything in the bathroom, Bill?"

"Just a foot-long floater in the bowl," he said. Everything was a joke to Bill, and the jokes were always foul or negative. They made David and me laugh sometimes, but not often. Ed enjoyed Bill's comedy about as much he would enjoy removing a tick with a burning-hot spoon.

"As long as you didn't take it, sticky-fingers," he replied.

Bill had been busted house-lifting twice by Ed. First he was caught taking jewelry from some old maid's ballerina box. Then, in another house, he swiped photos the tenant there had taken of his girlfriend. They were as nasty as anything you'd see in Hustler. One more strike and Bill was out. Not free of patrolling, though. He would have liked that. Instead Bill would be reassigned, which almost always meant clean-up duty, mopping up mangled corpses in a demolished city. Ed held that threat over Bill's head like hangman's noose whenever Bill got cranky or too sarcastic, and it always shut him right up.

Ed turned to me.

"You find anything in the garage, Hank?"

"Not a body. Not even a car. I reckon these folks evacuated when the news hit."

"Yeah, it looks like most of Yeehaw jumped on the turnpike," he replied. "But we've got to be sure. Search the kitchen. David, get the other bedrooms, and Bill, hit the other head."

Ed began jotting down notes in his log and the three of us separated. We always stuck pretty close to each other in case of an attack, but most of the time if a zombie was in a room, you wouldn't even have time to enter it 'cause it'd come charging out at you. Once you walked into the house, they knew you were there. So if we came through the front door OK, we broke up and searched to save time. We'd individually find part-timers, but if they hadn't already lunged at us, then they were starting to recover, which meant that they'd be so sick they'd be slower than cement.

I entered the kitchen, and the whole look and feel of the room made me sentimental. I instantly longed for the simpler, better times, before the plague. You rarely came across rooms like this when scouting. Most places were a mess. You could always tell that either violence had occurred, or people had dashed out in a mad panic, leaving behind tornadic wreckage in their haste. But this kitchen looked as if the owners had just gone out to pick up milk and would be back any minute.

There were curtains on the window that were decorated with a soft flower pattern. The fridge was an old, brown model with silver handles, and pots and pans hung above the stove on a magnetic strip. The wallpaper was vertical stripes, and an oversized wooden fork and spoon set hung on the wall by a Girl Scouts calendar. In the middle of the room was a small, wooden table with a big, open cookie jar in the center. The floor was old yellow tile, and two doggie bowls were plopped down on a big mat that said "*Dolly.*"

That's when I heard the howling.

There was a screen door near the fridge, leading out to the backyard. The window on it was up, and a muggy wind blew in, making the curtain dance like forgotten laundry on the line. Carried on that wind was the sound of the howling, coming from somewhere in the yard.

Normally we'd investigate any noises as a group. But after seeing the Dolly mat and the bowls, I had gotten excited when I heard the howling. I wondered if the family had left the dog behind for some reason, as sad as that would have been. I was happy to imagine that I might adopt her if only I found her first. I thought I'd get dibs that way. A dog wasn't like jewelry or naked pictures; it would have to come back with us. And if one did, I wanted it to be mine. No arguments or paper-rock-scissors, just mine.

I went out into the yard. The howling had stopped, but there was a yip and a yelp, like playful barking. But all I saw was brown crabgrass and some withered vegetable plants drooping in their bone-dry pots. A rustling of palmetto bush led me toward the woods behind the house, which really was more a mesh of vine and shrub than trees. The yelping got louder as I came forward, expecting to see a pup, but instead I got her.

She was a foul-looking lil' zombie, full-blown. She couldn't have been more than 7. Her blond hair was still in pigtails, tied with pink bows at the end. Her eyes were glossed over like they get when you've got the sickness, and her mouth was a mess of fractured teeth, all jagged and chipped from gnawing on bones. Her skin was the color of fetid swamp-bog, and the reek of her putrefaction could knock a maggot off a turd.

She could have jumped at me in the usual frenzy, but instead she yipped and yapped at me, still making the puppy noise. When I looked down at her little buckled shoes, I knew why. She was squatting there over a furry, bright-red pulp with fangs and a black snout sticking out at one end. Hung around a pile of this gore like a sad halo was a leather collar with poor Dolly's name engraved on it.

This little Zombina already had herself a meal, and something about it registered in what was left of her brain, making her yap like a puppy. The sight of all this jolted me, even though I'd seen my share of horror since Z1V1 first hit. I wanted to vomit, but calmed my gut down to a belch and then started to steady my rifle. But this ghoulie-girl had a belch of her own brewing, and when I turned back to shoot her, she burped a mist of dark blood with such force that it sprayed all over my face. My eyes started to burn as my mouth tasted the nauseating copper, and for a moment I couldn't see, but I shot anyway.

* * * * *

By the time David got over to me, I had wiped my face clean with a sanitizing wipe from my bag. I was still spitting out what I hoped was only dog blood, but I was prone to having a cheek full of Redman, and I think he was so used to me dippin' that he didn't really notice. I was glad he didn't, because I was damn scared.

"Good God," he sighed when he saw the remains of the girl lying there in that puddle of a dog.

"God ain't got nothing to do with this," Ed said, coming up behind him. I noticed his pistol was drawn. "You OK there, Hank?"

"Yeah, just rattled."

"You should have called for us before going back outside."

"Sorry, Ed. I just thought we were in the clear."

My eyes felt like someone had poured Tabasco sauce in them. I rubbed at them with the back of my hand. Even through the blur, I could make out Ed's curious expression.

"You sure you're OK?"

"I'm fine, fine. Just the damn dry air."

David handed me a jug of water, and I splashed it onto my face, trying to wash out my eyes without looking like that was what I was doing. Bill came walking up as I did, and I was grateful for the distraction.

"What's all the hubbub, Bub?"

"Hank found a full-blown one. Be on your toes."

The one thing Bill did take seriously was a zombie. He armed himself and went silent, scanning the surrounding brush. I was worried about more of them ghouls being around too, because they tended to move in packs, like coyotes prowling on garbage night. But beyond being worried about them, I was now even more worried about myself. That little Zombina had hosed me good with all kinds of fluid: blood, spit, bits of mucus, and who knows what else, all from the mouth of a zombie. I had not heard of the virus being spread this way, but it made sense to me that it would be possible. But I surely didn't want to ask David and find out. I didn't want him or Bill to know, and I damn sure didn't want Ed to have any inkling. I'd end up tagged and shipped off to one of those rehabilitation centers that were all so overcrowded, packed in there with all those part-time cannibals, screaming and thrashing all night long with raging sickness.

Because there was nothing to do for it once you had it. There was no cure or painkiller to ease you through or help you recover faster. You just had to ride that mean sucker to the end like a roller coaster that you wished you'd never hopped onto to begin with. Like the flu, you just had to sweat it out, and like a junkie going cold turkey, the hunger was supposed to be a living nightmare.

I didn't want to end up like that. I didn't want to turn into a zombie either, but I didn't want to go to rehab. I hadn't been bitten, and so I wanted to think that I would be fine. So I told myself I would be, and then I tried my darnedest to believe it.

* * * * *

There's a feeling of uncertainty that you get sometimes when drinking or doing dope, that moment when you wonder if it's working. That's why there are so many drunk-driving arrests. Folks aren't sure if they're sauced, and they talk themselves into believing they're sober. The very fact that they have to contemplate it should tell them that the booze has had an effect. But alcohol and dope make you trick yourself, and I reckon the virus does that too.

The day after I got puke-sprayed by that undead brat, I started asking myself if I felt any different. I would run my hands through my hair just for the sensation, and then I'd wave my fingers in front of my face and snap them in my ears. Of course, the only surefire test would be to sneak a vial from David's medical kit, but even if I could manage to swipe the equipment without being caught, I doubted I could use it correctly. I'd seen the kid administer the test plenty of times, but I wouldn't trust myself to do it right. I'd just end up with the same fears and doubts I was already suffering from.

"You doin' all right?" Ed asked as I ran my hand through my hair again.

"Yeah, why?"

My bowels churned at the question.

"You just seem a little off," he replied. "Can't say I blame ya, either. Zombie kids are the worst. It's a damned vile thing to see, and then it never leaves your mind's eye."

I began to fear the concern of my teammates and see it as their subconscious way of admitting that they suspected me of infection. I tried to shrug it off as sheer paranoia, a delusion brought on by post-traumatic stress, insufferable heat and too much dehydrated food. But the fear was there now, germinating within me. The only thing stronger than the fear was the hunger. It was so fathomless that it crept out of my guts and strained my bones till they ached. It festered in me and grew worse when I tried to satiate it. I'd scarf down jerky or a protein bar as we marched through the streets, and it would only make me hungrier, as if my stomach was insulted by this offering. That night we ate our dinner rations as usual, and I tucked mine into my sleeping bag when no one was looking, knowing that the meal would only cause pain.

I lay down to sleep early, telling myself I had indigestion, or maybe acid reflux. I told myself it would pass, and yet I still kept it all a secret from my team, because deep down I think I knew it was something more. My heart sank like an anchor at the thought, so I tried to think of nothing as I lay there staring into a sky without stars.

* * * * *

"Hey, you awake there, or what?"

It was Bill. We were on our 12th day of patrol now. We were scouting behind a convenience store, and I had zoned out again, staring at the back of his ear. The flesh there was spongy and pink, the lobes appearing to have the chewy texture of gummi worms but the savory flavor of pork ribs.

"Huh?" was all I could offer as a reply at this point.

Bill snickered at my spaced-out manner.

"Listen, hoss," he said. "If you've got some cheba or somethin' else that makes this daily grind more bearable, it'd be great if you didn't bogart it."

He came closer to me, and the stink of his sweaty flesh was as alluring as any lady's perfume I'd ever smelled. We were alone in the back alley with the dumpster and crates, Ed and David searching the insides of the store. The intimacy was like that between a jungle cat and a small, unwitting marmot: Only one of us was really aware of the dangerous dance. I could feel my mouth salivating as my stomach seemed to implode.

"Come on, brother," he said. "Don't hold out. Give it to me."

I looked into his eyes and thought of sucking them out of his skull and juggling them with my tongue like a hacky sack. There was garlic on his breath, so his tongue would be well-seasoned. I wondered if his teeth would pass through me whole if I swallowed them.

"I don't even care what it is," he said, "just as long as it takes me away from here."

It was more than an urge. It was like a reflex.

I had my rifle, a knife, a box cutter, and plenty of other things I could have used as a weapon. But the mechanical advantage is calculated by the mind of man, and I wasn't operating on that wavelength any longer.

I went at Bill with my mitts.

I think he would have screamed if he'd only had the time. I moved with a speed that was unfamiliar to my body, lunging at him like an Olympic diver. I knocked him backward in a tackle, and he hit the gravel with a crack, the air escaping his lungs as his spine snapped on impact. There was no hesitation then. I went face first into his neck, chewing, tearing away the sinew in huge strips. I didn't just eat the flesh — I inhaled it. The eating was a delirious frenzy of blood mist and meat so fresh it was still steaming. I don't remember really thinking about what I was doing. There certainly wasn't any feeling of shame, remorse, or even uncertainty. I wasn't even afraid of being caught by the others. The only feelings I had were of satisfaction and relief, like a morphine addict getting back on the nod.

However, you know, the flesh wasn't quite enough.

I began to pulverize his skull by bashing it into the ground. I dug my thumbs into his eye sockets for a good grip and wrapped my fingers around his head. I whacked his skull on the fractured gravel over and over again — like trying to bust a stubborn coconut. But my strength, like my speed, had been elevated, and soon the back of his skull split open with a little hiss, and I was able to start prying the halves apart. His brain spilled out, bloody but intact, like a newly born baby, right into my grip.

The taste of it was like French kissing an angel.

In less than a minute, I had consumed Bill's entire brain. Trying to go back to his mere flesh after that delicacy was suddenly unthinkable. Besides, he was already starting to seem less appetizing to me. While still a warm new kill, he was suddenly unappealing now. It was like pancakes — the first bite was divine, but each additional bite was less and less appealing, until it just made you retch.

But then there was the brain. Sweet Mary and Joseph, there was that divine brain. I cannot ever begin to emphasize the otherworldly ecstasy of chomping down into that pulpy mass. It was like an orgasm for the soul, like a religious experience bathed in gory bliss.

I stood up then and stared down at Bill's hollowed-out skull. I remember thinking to myself: *Betcha can't eat just one*. I laughed at this, snorting, sending shards of Bill trickling out of my nostrils. Crawling into the dumpster, I closed the lid over me, letting it rest on top of my head. This left just enough room for me to see and for the business end of my rifle to pass through. The dumpster was half-full of garbage that was months old, and the stench of it was now like a botanical garden to my blood-encrusted sinuses. As I crouched there in the filth, circling through my head like a song you cannot shake was the sound of that little ghoulie girl, just yap-yap-yapping like a brain-dead pup.

* * * * *

They tried calling us on the walkie-talkies first, but I wasn't answering, and Bill was in no condition to. So I steadied my rifle, knowing they'd be coming around the bend shortly. My hands shook, as did my whole body. Even my teeth ground together as I smiled at the thought of more skulls to split. The impulse to catapult myself out of the dumpster and just lunge at them was hard to fight. But I was still cognizant enough to know that Ed would have blasted me to bits before I could peel off his face with my incisors. My stomach played Twister with itself and bile danced at the back of my throat, the hunger pulsing harder now with each minute I went without human flesh. But I held fast to my resolve, like any good foot soldier would have. With Bill, I had just pounced, with no thoughts of tools or strategy. But now that I had eaten, the compulsion that came with the hunger wasn't as overpowering. I had regained a bit of self-control, no matter how small.

Expecting the worst after getting no reply from us, Ed and David crept around the edge of the building with guns drawn. The sheen of Ed's police issue was like a diamond in the relentless sunlight. His eyes went right to Bill, of course, ignoring the dumpster. That was all the time I needed to plant a bullet in his chest. The crack of my rifle echoed several times in the still of the afternoon, and Ed fell backward into David, who screamed and dropped his pistol as he, too, fell. David paged for backup assistance on his walkie-talkie, whereas Ed was much more gung-ho in his self-defense. I had aimed for his heart, but my tremors had thrown off my aim, and there was still some life in the old lawman. He began to fill the dumpster with rounds, and I felt a hot slug enter my right shoulder and another skim my thigh, tearing the skin without going in. I bolted upright at the shock, lifting the lid and exposing myself. When Ed saw me, he became disoriented by it, not expecting a member of his team to be the attacker. This second of hesitation was all the advantage I needed to shoot him right through the neck. His jugular burst open like a geyser.

David was screeching his location to the dispatcher when I fell on him. His soft, young flesh was like a freshly powdered baby. I remember wondering if his high IQ would make his brain sweeter than Bill's. I cracked his skull like a walnut with the butt of my rifle, and then fell into his scrambled brains as if they were a lover's arms.

* * * * *

The backup unit found me with all three of my team members' carcasses stacked around me like a human buffet. I had made a temple of their savory corpses, each of them propped up against a different side of me, with myself in the middle, caked in their blood and festooned in their innards, feasting in a frenzy that escalated with every bite.

It was mere luck that saved me. The team leader of this particular squadron was one of those liberals bent on reconstructing humanity. She'd rather let a raving zombie escape than shoot a part-time cannibal. Had it been someone like Ed, he would have turned me into soup with the amount of lead he would have pumped into me. He was by the book, but he valued safety overall. This team leader, though, was on some kind of crusade, and so she had me zapped with a taser and then netted so that a proper test could be administered.

The test came back negative. I had reached the height of the sickness but my cells were already showing signs of recovery. The medic noted that my skin tone hadn't gone gray. He said my fever was bound to break by nightfall, and that after two days in confinement he'd expect me to realize what I had done, and then the true therapy would begin, because the remorse of a part-time cannibal was known to be one of mankind's most terrible burdens.

But I, like all of you, beg to differ.

I spent several months in a crowded rehab facility and made a full recovery. Once they deemed me as being no threat to others, they pulled me from the crowded cells and put me into the ward. There, in those warm and fuzzy group sessions, I slowly came forward with the story I have just shared, and made sure to have my own signature breakthrough where I accepted that because of the virus, I was a victim. I abandoned all ownership of the horrible things I had done, and found forgiveness among my peers, within myself, and in the eyes of Christ.

Or so I told the counselors, because I knew what they wanted to hear.

Many of you in this gathering tonight, I met in the ward. Others I met in those hellish holding cells. The rest of you are friends of those friends, and I can see tonight that our group is growing. We aren't zombies, but we aren't part-time cannibals either, now, are we?

Each of us here tonight has walked upon the tightrope that hangs taut over the chasm of death, and we have each stared lovingly into it and felt its heavenly embrace. We all know the salvation that lies within the flesh, and we alone have felt the kiss of God on our lips when we have feasted, and *only* when we have feasted.

Ours is a religion founded upon that glimpse of the borderland between our world and the world beyond. We are *The Great Eaters*. This zombie virus has given birth to a new era — not the Armageddon so many viewed it as, but rather a long Last Supper. The bodies are indeed temples, and they welcome us in the most Christian manner of all, crying out to us, saying: *"This is my body, given for you."* It is not bread, but the actual body. It is not wine, but the blood itself. There is no *transubstantiation*, but rather a *transmutation* that we all must experience to compel us to first taste the divinity found in human devourment. We did not succumb to the plague, nor did we shy away from its teachings, unable to handle the burden of sacrifice like the part-timers. We, my brethren, are the chosen ones.

I have no doubt that you've noticed the pine box behind me as I have given you my confession and this sermon. Brothers Larry and Daniel have brought us this offering of communion rite. This vessel was but a girl of 14 when she died, and she was exhumed from the cemetery the very night of her burial, which was only last night. She has not been tainted by the devil's embalming fluid, but frozen before her burial instead. She's been thawed now, and I have used my slaughterhouse learning to prep her for mass.

May we all gather around this blessing now, and humble ourselves before we once again glimpse the threshold of Heaven. Bow your heads, my beloved brethren. It is time to say grace.

Growing Dark

Beyond the rusting fence, the fallow land looked ashen to Billy. This barren soil, which Pa had decided to let rest from cropping, wore the same gray death mask as the sky that sulked above the farm like a swollen pustule. He found it hard not to lose himself in Halloween daydreams when autumn fell to gloom like this, but there was little that didn't distract Billy from his chores. It wasn't that he didn't want to work — far from it. There was nothing he desired more than to prove himself to his old man. But no matter the task at hand, farm work was never engaging enough to keep his mind from floating off into fantasies. Pa had scolded him about it many times: Billy was 11 years old now and needed to quit his head-tripping if he was ever going to become a man.

Remembering this, he got back to the sheep. He sat on the stool behind Holly, one of their ewes, and used scissors to clip the dags from around her anus. These were clumps of fur that had been stitched together with shit, forming rank pendants that Billy thought looked like the tears of a giant. If the dags weren't clipped, they could lure maggots. Holly could get infested, and if she did, Billy knew Pa would send him marching into the sugarcane to cut a switch to be beaten with. His behind was still sore from when he'd let Rosey, one of the junker cows, mix in with the good ones during a milking. He hadn't even caught the auger before the old man had started whooping his hide for that goof.

He'd been daydreaming then too, he had to admit to himself.

He continued clipping the smaller dags, doing all he could to stay focused even as he felt the first drops of rain. He didn't care if he got drenched and his wranglers grew as heavy as a throw rug — he was going to finish tending to the sheep, and Pa would be proud, he just knew it.

With Holly taken care of, he herded some of the other ewes that bore what Pa called *love stains* on their backsides. They'd raddled the big ram, Buck, and now when he mounted one of the ewes, the harness on him marked the ewe with red paint so they knew which of them still needed time with the ram. Pa had been grumbling about how Buck was shooting duds of late, but Billy didn't know what that meant, and he knew better than to question the old man. He just herded the sheep and was happy to be trusted with that, or anything else on the farm. It helped convince him that he wasn't totally hated.

Spooked by sudden thunder, the Clydesdales in the stable bucked. They were always restless when they didn't have to drag a chain hallow. Billy's initial reaction to this was to play with them a little and maybe break up a carrot. He loved all the animals on the farm, but he felt that he had a special kinship with the horses and the cattle. He wanted them to have peace in their hearts; if not serenity, than at least the soft calm that Billy himself so longed for. But he fought the urge to coddle them, knowing it to be just the sort of thing that would distract a woman but should never keep a man from his work.

Atop the barn, a murder of crows burst into a fluttering tornado at the approaching rain. The sheep's ears spun on their skulls like crippled butterflies. Behind the chicken wire, a fat hog belched a horrid squeal. The whole of the livestock began to twitch with their convoluted emotions.

Billy Joe became too curious to restrain himself anymore. He looked up at the growing clouds, and then at his animal friends.

"Ya'll know somethin', dontcha?" Billy asked them, smirking.

He sprinted to the fence where the hog frothed.

"What is it, boy?" he asked. "Werewolves, goblins, Martians?"

His mind bloated with images, visions based on monsters he remembered from a comic that one of the laborers had given him. He'd hidden it under his mattress in his herder's shed, and by now had memorized every line. Even as he wandered deeper into his right-brained escapades, he began to pet the swine, which snorted in reply. He began to daydream of being a shining knight, the kind that Momma used to tell him fairy stories about. He envisioned himself with all the muscular definition of one of the Clydesdales, but shrouded in shimmering chain mail. He could see himself on top of one of those very horses, galloping after some shape-shifting villain in the light of a phantom moon. He began to rap his hands upon the hog's snout, creating the sounds of the trotting steed in his fantasy.

Later, alone in his shed, he would wonder how Pa always managed to catch him at these moments, no matter how few or far between.

"Where is that boy that looks after the sheep?" he heard the gravel voice bark from behind him.

It was Pa, cruelly reciting that rancid rhyme, the one that Momma used to sing to him at bedtime when he was little. The sweetness of it was long gone, though, for Pa used it now to point out just how little Billy still was. It was a mocking, ridiculing poem in the old man's mouth, and he spat it out like a cobra hissing venom.

"Under a haystack," Pa continued, "fast asleep."

* * * * *

Judson had fetched his boy because the rain was coming down harder now, and he didn't need Billy Joe falling ill after working in it, or at least farting around with the goddamned pigs. One sickly mouth was more than enough for his house, especially since he'd been forced to cut back on the day laborers. The doctor bills had become like a vise, and he needed what little kin he had to be healthy if the blasted farm was to meet quota, especially now that it was harvest time.

"I took care of all the dags, Pa," the boy told him.

"There's more to herding than plucking dingleberries, boy."

Judson clanked the plates so the noise echoed throughout the tiny kitchen, driving home his aggravation. *Damned kid.*

"Yes, sir, but I sorted the herd too. Buck's mounted a few of the ewes since we raddled him."

Judson threw a full plate on the table between them. He pointed at Billy with a mean closeness to his nose.

"Listen to me, boy," he croaked. "When I came out there, all I saw was your monkey hands playing a hog's head like a bongo. I don't need no dillydallying on my farm, and I don't take kindly to no goldbricking leeches living on it. You need to pull your head out of Fairyland and start earning your keep, sonny."

The boy lowered his gaze, the shame weighing on him. He went to sit at the table, pulling the plate full of cornbread and cold cutlets toward him as if it was his own. Judson slapped his son's wrist and winced with disgust as he saw the boy pull his paw away like a frightened pup.

"That ain't your grub, boy!" he barked. "Hell's bells, don't you know better by now?"

"Sorry, Pa. I just forgot."

"That's 'cause you don't pay no attention. Now bring Momma her lunch before you go eatin' your own."

* * * * *

The floorboards seemed to bend more and more whenever he climbed the steps. Billy stopped and checked over his shoulder for Pa. The old man wasn't at the bottom of the stairs, so he thought it would be okay to take a second to inspect them. He placed the plate at the top of the stairs and bent down to get a better look at the rotting wood. There was black fuzz hiding between the cracks. He'd been noticing it in the folds of the farmhouse. He scratched some away and watched a small trickle of black liquid release, like blood from a torn scab. But that quiet scraping was just enough to wake her.

He heard moaning from behind the doorway. It was a sound so horrible to him that it made the hog's braying sound like bluegrass. A phlegmy hacking that chilled him followed the cry. And although he couldn't see it, he knew that the phlegm would be pink with blood when he went inside.

Picking up the plate, he made his way to the door and opened it. From the smell, he knew there was something in the bedpan for him. The light was always kept dim because of her sensitive eyes, but with the storm outside banishing all sunshine, the room was now a catacomb. He moved forward slowly, putting the plate on the table beside her bed.

She turned to him, and even in the muted light he could make out the sunken pits of her eyes. She'd grown so thin that her cheeks looked like two perfect eggshells. A small sliver of gray light knifed through the parted curtain and reflected off of the long row of stitches that ran from her forehead to her collar. What little hair she had left could no longer cloak it.

"Billy Boy," she whimpered, reaching out to him.

These days, whenever Momma spoke, it sounded like crying. He didn't know how to put it into words, but he wished she could *fake it* in front of him. He wished she could force herself to sound less like she was dying when he was around. If anything, he felt like she fed off his pity, and then he hated himself for thinking something so rotten about his momma. He often scolded himself, unknowingly using his father's voice to tell himself he was just making excuses not to take care of her. But that wasn't true. The truth was simple, and sad enough: He didn't like seeing her this way. It was abhorrent. In all honesty, he hardly even recognized her as the warm woman who had raised him.

The sickness had taken no time at all to transform her from a caring matriarch into this disintegrating alien, and Billy had been rushed through stages of grief that he didn't understand, his empathetic nature turning on him. All he knew now for sure was that he needed to be a man about this. That meant that he wasn't supposed to cry, so when he had to, he did it alone, curled up on the hay-stuffed mattress in his shed.

"My sweet Billy Boy," she said, stroking his cheek. He reached up to hold her withered hand. It had once been so plump, and now it was just like a sheet of moth-eaten silk draped over a skeleton. He stroked it carefully, afraid of tearing a vein. In this gentle moment, they remained so silent that they could hear the old house settling. Billy Joe heard the creaks and pops within the walls and thought again of the black moss, wondering if it lay somewhere beneath, hiding behind the world he could not see, bleeding blackly as it started swallowing his family like so much sunshine.

* * * * *

The early light was still pale, and his fatback had not yet settled in his belly, but Billy was already toiling in the field. The hairs of some of the corn had turned brown, and so Pa had shucked one just to be sure, poking the kernels with his toothpick. It looked to Billy as if the corn was giving up milk. Pa had told him the row was ripe for plucking, and so they'd gone to work.

Billy had harvested enough to fill a wheelbarrow before he tripped over the thorny vines of the acorn squash Pa'd planted to keep the varmints away. He broke his fall with both hands, skidding across the pricks and skinning his palms. The pain brought tears to his eyes. It wasn't an emotional reaction, just a physical one, but he was nonetheless terrified. Pa was only a few feet away.

He turned around, putting his back to the old man. He spit into his bloody hands and worked the saliva into the cuts to soothe them. The flesh rolled away. He heard his father shuffling behind him, and in his panic he destroyed the evidence by quickly eating his skin.

"What's the holdup, son?" Pa asked.

"Sorry, Pa. Just tripped on a root there. I'm fine."

He went right back to the corn and started shucking, but the old man wasn't dumb. He scowled and grabbed Billy's wrists, turning his hands palms up. Billy had balled them into fists.

"Open them mitts before I box your ears."

Billy did as he was told and closed his eyes. After a moment he heard Pa telling him: "Get inside and wash these out. We don't want no infection neither, so swab them wounds good with the iodine. We got some bandages in the bathroom cupboard. Wrap yourself on up, and then get back outside, you hear?"

"OK, Pa."

"More work is what you need," he told him.

With that, the old man raised his hands up and showed Billy his palms, which were as rough and leathery as an old saddle.

"Keep on working, boy," he said. "You keep skinning off that baby fat, and one day you'll have the respectable hands of a man."

* * * * *

By the time Billy had returned to the field, it was close to eight o' clock. The migrant workers had arrived and were harvesting, so Pa sent him on to milk the cows. On the way, he threw feed to the chickens and tried not to daydream. When he got inside the barn, one of the cattle, a big bossy named Bertha, mooed at him. She'd always been affectionate and liked to lick at him with her sandpaper tongue. Pa liked to say that she'd been true to her name 'cause she'd birthed them some busk calves, which Pa had sold at weaning.

Billy knew in his mind that she was crying out to be milked, but in his heart he imagined that she missed her babies. He started to pet her, careful of his wrapped hands. She responded right away, nuzzling him. He opened the partition and went in, sitting beside her. Her udders were swollen and dripping, the veins as thick and hard as grapevines. She ached to be milked, and it showed.

At first he wasn't very surprised by the sight of blood in her milk. He knew that it was common enough after calving. But as he continued to pump, the fluid turned to more blood than milk, and it began to flow steadily even as he stopped pumping all together; it began to gush out of Bertha, the discharge turning dark purple as it fled from her body. Billy stood and stepped back as the bossy began to bellow, and the hay at his feet blackened as the dirt floor turned to mud.

He covered his mouth so as not to scream.

* * * * *

With Bertha in the trailer, he and Pa took the old Ford up to see Uncle Merle at the knacker's yard. It was a professional slaughterhouse with state-of-the-art machinery, unlike the shack they had behind the barn — which Pa referred to as *The Lil' Abattoir*, smirking every time he said it as if he was some sort of sophisticate. But they called Merle's workplace a knacker's yard for a reason. It was not the place to go if you wanted meat suitable for eating. Billy knew where they were taking Bertha, and why, and it simply made him sick inside.

Why couldn't it have been Rosey? he thought. She wasn't just a junker, she was dumb, and mean to boot. He wouldn't miss her like he would ol' Bertha.

They pulled up at the rear of the building and got out of the pickup. When they opened up the trailer, Pa pulled Bertha out, her bell clanking loudly and echoing in the small confine. Billy swallowed back a bit of rising bile when he saw the floor of the trailer, caked in the darkest blood he'd ever seen. A throng of black flies swarmed around her like a curse, and it was all they could do to shoo even half of them away. Uncle Merle came out of the building, and Billy couldn't help but think that he looked like a mad scientist. He wore a shiny apron that was slick with gore and a pair of goggles strapped to his head. He was slathered in sweat, and an unlit cigar shifted from one corner of his mouth to the other.

He took one look at Bertha and snorted.

"Lord, Judson, this is one sorry-looking beast."

"Yeah, but she's big. A lot of meat on this one," Pa replied.

Uncle Merle had a voice like a grizzly, and a face to match. He wasn't mean to Billy, but he was gruff. He was a thick brute of a man, and Billy feared him almost as much as he did Pa. He'd been told all his life that Merle was his Momma's older brother, but he could never bring himself to believe that they were related. He had a hard enough time accepting that Merle was even human.

"Look at the blood pissing out of her," Merle said. "I doubt she's well enough to have her chops pass for dog food. She's fertilizer at best."

Pa squinted, the folds of his face deepening.

"Just make me an offer, Merle, and remember I have your dying sister in my loft."

Merle didn't have a snappy retort, so he looked down at Billy and ruffled his hair. He frowned at the bandages on his hands.

"What in tarnation happened to you now, boy? Stigmata?"

"No, sir. Just skinned myself shuckin'."

Merle turned back to his Pa and asked "Why'd you bring him here, anyway?"

"I thought it'd be good for the boy to see it done proper."

Merle's face fell slack.

"Come off it, Judson," he said. "This ain't no place for a wee boy."

"He's almost 12," Pa barked back. "But he still has a lot of growing up to do. I thought a dose of the real deal would get his head out of the clouds and his thumb out of his backside."

"I've just been prying out tallow and lard for the rendering plant. Ain't nothin' to see in there but buckets of waste product."

"But we've got this bossy right here. I thought the boy could help slaughter her."

Billy gulped and shuddered all at once. He felt the tears building up. They were emotional this time, and he didn't know how well he could hold them back.

"Jud …"

"Jud nothin'," Pa said. "You get the first grab at every bit of unfit livestock I have. All I'm asking is that you show your nephew here the trade, and maybe help him man up in doing so."

There was a pause filled only by the macabre symphony coming from behind the metal sheen of the slaughterhouse. Merle shook his head.

"It's mechanical now," he said. "We don't even use the bolt pistols here. We send 300 volts through them before they're killed. I can't let a kid operate that kind of equipment."

"You still use a knife, though, don't ya?"

"Yeah."

"Well, the boy knows how to use one of those right proper."

Beside him, Billy felt Bertha nuzzle his armpit. He tilted his head, hoping the tears would sink back into his eyeballs. Above them, the tree branches rocked in the breeze, the dead leaves dropping off as mementos of a more innocent summer, now gone.

Merle took the rope that hung from Bertha's collar.

"I'll get her set up. Meet me inside in a few minutes."

* * * * *

The corridors of the knacker's yard were cold and metallic, as unfriendly as a museum. Large men in bloody aprons walked along steel grates carrying tools he didn't recognize, and it seemed that everywhere he looked there was a mangled mess of meat. When they entered the main hall, the pale carrions that hung by hooks from one long girder mystified Billy. They didn't resemble animals or meat, but some morbid hybrid of the two. What he did recognize, however, was the massive cow that hung from its hind legs over a big bowl. Its throat was slashed, and it was offering a crimson waterfall.

They entered the chamber where his uncle was with Bertha. She was standing at the base of a metal square that clamped her on either side of her neck, keeping her head locked inside of it. Her eyes stared deep into him, looking like two black planets, gleaming.

"What is this?' he asked, wincing at the whimper he heard in his voice.

"Your uncle is gonna stun Bertha, son," Pa told him. "Once she's brain-dead, we can string her up and you can bleed her yourself, like a man."

"But, Pa ..."

"For God's sake, don't you start bawlin'. I need a man around that farm, not some sissy."

"Pa, don't make me ..."

"Damn it, Billy! When I was your age, I had to crack open cows' heads with a sledgehammer, and I had to do it when I was a lot younger than you are now. You wanna be a little boy forever? Spend all day long laying in a haystack, making pictures out of the clouds?"

"No, Pa, I just don't wanna kill Bertha. She loves me."

"She's too sick for you to love back, boy. A man's gotta do what a man's gotta do, love ain't go no part in it."

He began to hyperventilate, and the old man slapped him across the face.

"Now, Judson," Uncle Merle butted in, "this ain't no easy thing for a young'un. Maybe we'll do it some other time."

Pa was inches away from Billy's face, livid and baring his nicotine-stained teeth. His graying hair was on end like the spine of a mad dog, and his nostrils had little red bolts of lightning streaking across the skin.

"If you can't be a man, you're no damn good, boy," he snarled. "You're dead weight, just like your momma."

* * * * *

That night, Pa did not allow him any supper. He was only allowed in the house to clean the pots. The smell of the food was torturous to him, and he knew it was part of his punishment. He told himself that he had it coming. In the sink, his bandages washed off of his hands almost right away, but his wounds had scabbed up mighty fine, and the hot water felt good.

When he finished, he went to leave, to rest in his shepherd's shed and watch the flock, but he was puzzled by the sounds coming from upstairs. They weren't running-water sounds, but plops and splashing noises like you'd hear down at the wading pond.

He tiptoed up the steps to the bathroom, seeing that the door to it was half open. He crept up to the doorway, doing his best to hide in shadow. Had he not been so morbidly captivated by what he saw, he might have noticed that the wall he leaned against was infested with a slick, black moss. Burrowing within it were small insects, stampeding in a way that made the mold itself writhe.

Pa's back was to him, and he was leaning over the tub. Draped around his shoulders were the spindly arms of Momma, looking like ghoulish claws reaching out of a grave. They had a ghostly pallor and were covered with sores of a bottomless black, a color of such putrid finality that it stopped Billy's breath. As Pa continued to bathe her, he leaned her back against the tub. Billy could see the rest of her now: the scarecrow rib cage, the flesh so white that it gleamed almost purple, and the pendulous teats that hung like satchel handles. Her body was merely rancid carrion now. The beauty had been stolen, as if her very life force had been pilfered by some unseen poltergeist.

Billy looked upward to avoid the sight. His gaze landed upon the ceiling, which was a dead sea of mildew. He stared into it, not caring about being lost in daydream now, needing any distraction from this heartbreaking horror. He felt almost hypnotized by it, as if he were floating freely in its encompassing gloom. The black mold called to him, crooning in a seductive lure. It seemed to tell him to lose himself, to exit the prison of his body and his miserable farm-boy life. Billy shuddered then, for it was more than the desire for escapism, it was the baiting of something carnivorous, something he reckoned was stalking his home and plaguing his kin.

He snapped his gaze away and looked at his folks again. He couldn't explain it if he had to, and he didn't fully understand it as it was. But he felt the subtle, horrid resonances. The nuances of this waking nightmare danced around him like a halo of locust. He had not recognized his momma for some time, but now, seeing one side of his Pa's face and the tears that ran down it, he no longer recognized the old man either.

Momma was beautiful.

Pa didn't cry.

Where had his parents gone?

He turned around so as not to bear the sight of it any longer, and when he did his palm reached for the wall, finding the fuzz. It pulsed between his fingers and oozed a dark slime. He pulled his hand away as if it were a flame, convinced now that it was some black moss of sorrow, a harvester come for their very souls.

"You got them," he whispered to it, "but you ain't getting me."

* * * * *

The first strange thing Judson noticed was the absence of the cock's morning caw. It hadn't woken him at dawn, and he thought that odd, but one look at the empty whiskey bottle gave him the explanation. He rose from the sofa and felt his boozed brain bounce off his skull like a ricocheting cue ball.

He wandered to the window and noticed the stillness right away. The livestock tended to get a little rowdy come morning time, anticipating feed and labor, but today the farm seemed like a tomb. He didn't bother changing into his overalls. He was too perplexed by the eerie calm. He slipped into his boots and walked out.

He saw the chickens first, spread across their plot like a hurricane had ripped through. He winced at the high cost of this loss. Every damn one of them was shredded to pulp.

"Damn it!" he hissed, cursing first the pack of coyotes he assigned blame for the massacre, and then redirecting that anger toward the boy who should have taken notice from his shed.

He stepped into the coop and glowered. Upon bending down to inspect the mess, he noticed something peculiar: The chickens hadn't been mauled; they'd been pulverized. Judson walked from one to another, seeing the same thing. Their heads had been mashed to the texture of soup. He went to the edge of the coop and leaned on the plank, puzzled as he stared off toward the stable. It was then that he saw Paddy, one of his Clydesdales. The horse's head hung limply, its long neck resting on the bottom door. From the angle at which it was propped, it looked as if the blow had fractured its face, but its neck had been snapped on the ledge, forced by its own weight upon falling.

This wasn't some pack of coyotes. This was some sort of sabotage.

Probably one of those damn fruit pickers I had to lay off, he thought. *Goddamned savages!*

He sprinted toward the barn where he kept the cows, and gasped at the emptiness within. They were all locked in wooden partitions of their own. Had they been standing, like usual, he would have seen them. But he didn't, and that meant that they were all lying down. He crept up to the first crate gingerly, praying it wasn't so, but his prayers, as always, went unanswered.

The first bossy lay before him in her box, her face smashed in and her throat slit. Her left eye had popped and her lower jaw had been dislocated. Her tongue hung out as if she were lapping up the pool of her own blood.

One by one, Judson checked on the rest, finding that they'd all been turned into so much head cheese; each had met an identical fate. Panic began to seize his heart, and sweat beaded in every crevice of his body.

"Billy?" he cried out. Not knowing whether to feel anger or fear, he began to drown in both.

He raced toward where the sheep grazed, nearly tripping over the first carcass. He paid it no mind and hurtled past the other piles of wooly gore, terror thudding in his chest with the ferocity of a thresher as he spun through this valley of death.

"Billy!" he called out, louder this time.

He made it to the herder's shed where Billy slept and flung open the door with such force that it snapped the top hinge. He trembled at finding it empty. It made his bowels churn and his flesh go goose.

The boy must be hiding, he told himself. *He must be scared to death, and this time I don't blame him none.*

He turned, scanning the fields for any sign of his only child. The October sun cast elongated shadows that made puppetry of the fences and barbed wire. Judson saw ghosts now on crates and demons clawing at the broad side of the barn, while all about him the stench of fresh, hot death germinated.

He turned back toward the house in a mad run.

He lunged up onto the porch and burst through the front door, calling his son's name. Finding the kitchen as empty as the den, he rushed upstairs. After finding all the other rooms vacant, he finally went to the bedroom, not wanting to upset his wife but seeing no other option. He tried to calm himself before going in, wanting to ease her through this, to remain ever vigilant as the man of the house. If he could show composure, it would soothe her, and he knew that with the cancer eating her, she needed whatever hope he could give her, no matter how false it may be.

"Sarah?" he called to her as he entered the gloom.

The bedroom was always as dark as a morgue, and it bothered Judson that he could never see when he was in it. He moved forward and reached out to the lump he could make out on the mattress. The stink hit his nostrils like a sucker punch; the smell inside the room was worse than ever, copper-like and thick. He found himself holding his breath.

Where he expected her shoulder to be, he felt another shape. It took him a moment to realize that it was her ankle. He moved his hand along the base of her calf. For some reason, she was lying backward in bed. This puzzled him, because he knew she was too weak to make such a drastic shift.

"Sarah, are you all right?"

No answer.

He reached for the lamp by the bedside. Turning it on, he immediately wished that he hadn't.

She had been turned around because there were long gaps in the footboard of the bed. She'd lost enough weight that she'd shrunk, and her head could fit through one of those slots with a little pushing. Once the poles were around her neck, she'd been too weak to wiggle out. Her hands were draped across the headboard where she had clutched it. There were bloody scratches where she had clawed at it, breaking off her fingernails. Below her head was an old bucket. It had overflowed with her blood.

Kneeling down, Judson saw the square dent in the top of her head, the calling card of a sledgehammer's blow. He lifted her broken skull and saw the deep cut that ran along her throat, the very neck he had kissed and inhaled the sweet scent of just months before. Grief fought horror for control of him then, and the lump in his throat was suffocating. But toppling them both was the fear, for he had yet to find Billy.

* * * * *

The corn wasn't just brown and ready for the harvest. It was caked in a blackness that resembled gunpowder. Each time he crashed through some of the stocks, the black dust filled the air for a moment before vanishing.

He stopped cold when he came across his son's Wranglers lying in the row. They were slick with blood. His belt and boots lay just before them, and Judson realized that it was bloody footprints that he'd been trailing through the corn.

He started to sob even as he pulled back the hammer on his revolver.

Please, Lord. Not my son. Not my only begotten son.

He followed the splatters in the dirt to the end of the cornfield, where a small hill led to the stretch of open valley. It faced east, and the light of this awful new day blinded him so that he could only see a silhouette, one so still that he at first mistook it for a scarecrow, even if it was a bit short for one.

"Billy ..." he said, recognizing the boy.

His son stood before him on the peak of the dirt mound. He was naked, and his nubile body was taut against the backdrop of the tangerine haze. In his hands was a scythe that dripped so thickly that Judson could make out the outline of every drop.

Judson wasn't even aware of the pistol dropping from his hand.

"My God, boy. My God, what's happened?"

Judson wanted to run to his son, but something held him back.

"I'm not a boy no more, Pa. Don't you see?"

The lump in his throat returned, bigger now, a monstrosity.

"I've done it, Pa," the boy said with pride. "Done it proper, like a man. Like a real man."

Judson felt his legs give out, and he crashed to his knees, too numb with shock to feel the pain of the impact.

Lord, what have I done?

"Have I made you proud, Pa?" Billy asked, and Judson was frightened most by the lack of sarcasm in his voice. The boy was serious.

"The livestock, son ..." he began, but couldn't finish.

"To prove to you that I wasn't soft anymore. Not your Little Boy Blue."

"But son, your momma. Your momma that done raised you, that loved you so much ..."

He looked up to see a genuine look of befuddlement upon the boy's blood-smeared face.

"She'd grown too sick to love back, Pa," Billy said. "And a man's gotta do what a man's gotta do, love ain't go no part in it."

At the raising of the scythe, the crows hidden in the corn took flight as if it were their lives that were in danger and not Judson's. The movement shook more of the black dust from the husks as the boy stepped forward, and the last thing Judson saw before the blade entered his neck were his son's vacant eyes staring deep into him, looking like two black planets, gleaming.

Reunion

If nothing else, I'm glad we killed Donnie in January.

I can't stand to be in Florida at any other time of the year. The humidity works into my flesh and drives up into my brain like some damn parasite. It's one of the many reasons I so rarely return to this upturned bucket of alligator dung. The only reason I ever do visit is for Angie. One way or another, I find my way down here every January 30th. I tell myself that at least I'm escaping the snow, even if it is for a morbid ritual of sorts. But I know it hasn't got anything to do with snow, or even the ritual, really. It's just about Angie, just like everything always was.

"Every year you surprise me," she says. Her eyes glow under the streetlights, like a kitten's, shimmering with the same pale gold that bounces off the water in the pot-holes. For all her wounded beauty, Angie still stuns me, more so now than when we were kids, age being so good to her.

"Come on," I say. "You should know by now that I keep my promises."

"Does it still feel right to you, Hank?"

"I don't know that it ever did, sugar."

She looks away, guilt adding weight to her sigh.

"How's the babies?" I ask, letting her know I understand.

"Good. Kyle is gonna be 3 next month, and Fay has started to crawl."

"Rob?"

"He's good too. Making better money on the night shift. I don't see him as much, but we get by better."

I almost say that I'm just glad she doesn't have to do anything harsh to get the money, but I agreed last year not to bring up her stripping days no more.

"Well," I say, looking out at the shore, "I'm glad Rob's good too."

I've never met Rob. I sometimes wonder if he knows I exist, considering how much I know about him. We leave the parking lot and start making our way onto the boardwalk. The sea air is nicer than I remember, and the dried palm trees are noisy in the wind.

"So when are you gonna get married?" she asks.

"I have to fall in love first, don't I?"

"I guess you're too tough for that, huh?"

"Some might say."

"Would they be right?"

"Don't know."

I look at her. Her smile is like a lantern in the coal-black chambers of my rotten heart. I can't ever imagine having children of my own, but if I did, I'd want her to be their mother. It goes beyond any kind of concept of love, as far as relationships are concerned. Some would say she's the one that got away. But it's not that. Angie's like family. The only family I've got.

"You working?" she says, asking much more.

"I get by fine."

"Just not honestly."

"If I tried to be anything but what I am, that would be the lie."

"I worry about that."

"Don't."

"Can't be helped."

"Can't be changed either. A man's gotta work, and there's only one thing I've ever been good at."

She pulls her feathery bangs away from her eyes. They dance backward as the wind picks up, writhing like a snake when you take a shovel to its head. I can see the scar above her right eye. Fifteen years of creams have hardly made a difference. Angie hates it. Not because she's vain, but because it reminds her.

"It's a nice night tonight," she says. "We don't get many cool nights here."

"Yeah, I remember."

There's an awkward silence for a moment before she speaks.

"How much do you remember?"

"We're not quite there yet, you know. We still have some walking to do."

"I wish I could forget."

"It'd be easier if you ignored the anniversary."

"Respect for the dead, Hank."

She puts her hand in the nook of my arm, and we stroll like old lovers. Beer cans and burrito wrappers from the nearby fast-food joint lay half-buried in the sand. Nothing ever really changes in a place like Satellite Beach. The moonlight bounces off the shards of broken glass, just like it did that night when I was 19.

I had never done a deal with Jerry, but I knew about him. He was a few years older, much deeper in the shit than any of the rest of us. Donnie was our hook-up when it came to Jerry, 'cause Donnie's older brother knew him. He'd score a little cash from one end, and a little dope from the other. For Donnie, being the connection was sweet and relatively safe.

When Jerry had first started getting edgy that night, Donnie had tried to mellow him out, telling him that Angie and I were cool. Jerry had Angie confused with some girl he'd heard about who had narced on somebody from his old gang. Said she fit the description too well. When he said that, it'd seemed like his whole head itched. She started to say something to reassure him, and his butterfly knife came out quicker than a finger snaps. He went for her eye, and she bent away from the blade. He got her right above the eye, the knife ricocheting off the bone. I pounced on him without even thinking. The broken bottle was right there, and I knew it, but the thought wasn't in my head in that flashing moment of rage. I busted my knuckles into his teeth, and he stabbed at me, catching only a shred of my jacket. But I stumbled, and he used my momentum to knock me to the ground. Donnie actually tried to pull Jerry off of me, to his credit. But Jerry was big and Donnie just wasn't — and for that matter, neither was I.

Jerry turned the knife upside down to plunge it into me, and that's when the crack had echoed out across the beach. I heard a broken moan, and Donnie crashed into the sand without even trying to break his fall. Jerry had been distracted by it just long enough for me to grab that broken bottle and twist it deep into his neck, breaking glass off into his Adam's apple. I didn't know much about cutting throats at that point in my life, but I either got lucky or there's just no wrong way to do it, 'cause in no time at all Jerry was off of me, shaking and clutching his neck, which pumped out his blood like a geyser.

Angie was shaking too, the .38 in her hands still coughing up cordite. She was staring at Donnie, who was crumpled on the beach like some forgotten rag doll. He wheezed for every pained breath. She hadn't meant to shoot him; he'd just been too close to Jerry, and had to shoot at him cause he was about to stab her boyfriend.

I'd had no idea she'd been carrying a gun. It was one of her many secrets.

I walked up to her and took the pistol from her before she could drop it. For all the misery her life had slung at her beforehand, there was never pain in her eyes like this before. I saw it glowing, there in the moonlight. It's been there ever since.

Jerry went still. Donnie, however, was wheezing and grabbing his chest with blood-soaked fingers. She'd hit the poor bastard in a lung. Blood bubbled out of the corners of his mouth when he gasped for air. Angie started to cry. She'd been the toughest girl in the halfway house, and yet there she was, weeping like a Girl Scout with a wagon full of rained-on cookies.

I was young then, but I'd already learned that it's easier to live with something when you feel like you had no choice in the matter. I didn't want her to have to decide. So all I said was: "There's no good way out of this."

Angie looked away. Then I shot Donnie in the head.

I turned around and shot Jerry in the face, just to be sure.

It was all over a lousy 600 bucks' worth of cheap nose candy that was probably cut with talc anyway, a typical drug deal for people in their early 20s.

"Here's the spot," Angie says. "Remember how they had used pieces of palmetto bushes as extra posts for the police tape?"

"Yeah."

They'd never found anything they could use. Not that the lives of two low-life drug peddlers meant much to the local police anyway. We'd thrown the pistol into the Indian River and kept our mouths shut. Just another drug-related homicide.

"You know," she says, "I say this every time, but I think about Donnie every day."

"I know you do."

"I wish I didn't. I wish I could be like you."

"No you don't."

Angie thinks I'm stronger than her, somehow. But it's not strength. When I killed Donnie and Jerry that night, whatever remained of the little boy in me was also killed by my actions. No more smiles. No more tears. Once you've killed, you never feel the need or desire to do either.

Donnie and Jerry were the first men I had ever killed. The more lives you take, the less personal murder seems. But Donnie is Angie's first and last kill. That's why she can't shake loose the ghost. Whereas with me, well, it's funny how the poison can be the cure.

"I wish I could make it better, Hank," she says.

"It was an accident on your end, and I finished him out of mercy. The way his life was going, he would've ended badly anyhow."

"We can't know that for sure."

"His older brother's in prison for arson. His little sister started hooking a few years back. She's been missing for over a year, and nobody's even searching for her anymore."

"That's Donnie's kin. It don't mean it's Donnie too."

"Don't regret it."

"Why the hell shouldn't I?"

"Because him losing his life saved yours."

She looks at me, blinking, lost.

"You went straight that night, Angie," I say to her, touching her fingers, feeling Rob's ring there. "After that, there was no more dealing. No more drugs and thugs. If Donnie hadn't died, you may not even be here now. No home. No husband. No babies reaching for you, calling you 'Mommy.'"

She starts to cry just a little bit. It doesn't ugly her at all.

"You see," she says, and smiles, holding my hand, "this is why I need you here with me, Hank."

"I know," I tell her. "That's why I'll be here next year."

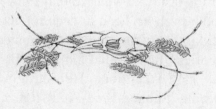

Before the Boogeymen Come

"I can't believe you pulled me out of the closet for this, Fred-Fred. The little brat's got his comforter on — you know damn well we can't get past protection like that!"

"Yeah," Fred-Fred admitted, his yellow fangs smiling on only one side of his mouth. "But ya see, his toes are exposed on his right foot. I thought maybe we could drag 'im out by them."

Meanie rolled his blood-red eyes in his oversized skull, smacking his furry forehead with his paw. He liked Fred-Fred well enough, but he was one of the dumbest goddamned Underbeds he'd ever lived next door to. Underbeds were notoriously dimwitted, but Fred-Fred was as empty-headed as a jack-o-lantern rotting on a stoop. While always well-intentioned, his plans to nab The Kid were always as half-cocked as a broken BB rifle and stupider than the tall tales The Old Lady would tell The Kid at night, just before it was time for Meanie, Fred-Fred and Slithers to get to work.

"Fred-Fred, you nimrod!" Meanie snarled. "Don't you remember the last time we tried that shit?"

Fred-Fred bowed his head in deep reflection, the bone and sinew of his brain hissing steam inside his lumpy cranium. Memories often evaded him, and this reference of Meanie's was no exception. He shrugged in reply. Frustrated, Meanie grabbed Fred-Fred's left arm. It was a fat log covered in purple, papilloma-riddled scales that seeped rank pus. He held it up to Fred-Fred's many eyes so that he could see the gnawed stump where his claw used to be. Now Fred-Fred remembered.

"Mr. Rex," Fred-Fred said in a sigh.

"That's right, pal. That little shit there keeps one of them stuffed puppies by his tootsies each night to protect him from ghouls like us. He already nabbed one of your talons there — don't let him run off with the rest of ya."

They both sighed now, looking at The Kid defiantly lying there in his bed with his Aquaman covers draped over him, snoozing away like they weren't even there. It was insulting to them at best, and threatening at worst. The deadline was drawing nearer, especially for Meanie. Fred-Fred figured that was why Meanie had been so irritable lately. Fred-Fred was worried too, but as a Monster Under the Bed he still had a few good years left with a 7-year-old boy. Slithers, being a Shadow Monster, still had time too, probably even more than he did. But Meanie was a Monster in the Closet. He was an old-school, hairy, goblin-like abomination. He was terrifying to young squirts but slowly became more laughable to them as they aged. Particularly because he lived in the closet, he would be the first to go, because the closet would have to make room for newer, different fears. It was only a matter of time before Meanie would be replaced by a boogeyman, some tall, male figure in black with a chalky face, often just a simple amalgam of cheap slashers from late-night movies the little brats would sneak a peek at.

"I'm sorry, Meanie. I just wanted to help. I've just been lying there at home with all them dust bunnies every night, worrying about the neighborhood and about our positions."

"Hey," Meanie said, "there ain't nothing to worry about here. I know we're short on time now, what with these kids maturing earlier and earlier, but we're good monsters, and we can get the job done."

"You don't think we're getting too old?"

"Why are you so negative all the time? We're not old, we're old-fashioned, and old-fashioned is good! We're the things that go bump in the night, the true classics. I keep telling ya, Fred-Fred, these zombie video games and teenage vampire sagas aren't going to steal our thunder forever. They're all just a fad. In the deep, dark of the night, we're still king shit."

Fred-Fred grinned wider. He liked seeing Meanie all riled up and brewing piss. For too many nights Meanie had just stayed in the closet, almost like he had given up. Fred-Fred was glad he had dragged him out tonight, even if his plan was as bad as they always were. At least Meanie was working again, basking in the pale moonlight by the edge of The Kid's bed.

"Well, we need to do something, gentlemen," a voice said from the chair in the corner. They turned and watched the small pile of clothing upon it suddenly transform into their neighbor, Slithers, the shape-shifting Shadow Monster. Tonight Slithers was comprised of dirty laundry, one of his more common forms. A long-sleeved shirt was wadded up for his head, two buttons forming his eyes and one sleeve slung forward at an angle to work as his mouth. His tongue was a soccer sock, long and yellow, with dirt stains on it. It hung out of his mouth as he spoke.

"I hate to alarm you," Slithers said, "but The Kid brought home a horror comic this evening. He must have borrowed it from a school chum. He's hiding it from his mum and dad, so we're in luck if they confiscate it before he reads it. Otherwise, he is going to have bigger, scarier things to cause him trepidation."

Meanie could not hide the consternation that flushed across his face like the surge of a urinal. Fred-Fred gulped, and Slithers waited for what he thought would be a hotheaded reaction, which was typical of Meanie's disposition. After all, he was an old-school monster, and his name suited him.

"What the hell are you worried about?" Meanie barked at Slithers. "You can change into whatever that little prick is scared of! Fred-Fred and I are the ones who'll be standing in the reassignment line!"

"The work ain't as available as it used to be, either," Fred-Fred said sadly.

"I fully understand the plight of our situation, good lads," Slither said. "I know I have a slight advantage, but I don't think it's fair to blame me for that. Besides, the way I see it is the way I always have: We are a team. If one of us has reason to worry, then we all do. As you said, Frederick, the monster market has shrunk in recent years. For prevention measures, children these days are so quickly exposed to real-life terrors like pedophiles and kidnappers that they hardly have the mind-set to imagine anything supernatural to be afraid of. Add to this the multiple avenues they have for hardcore horror entertainment, and it is no wonder that spookies like ourselves are becoming obsolete."

"You sure talk good," Fred-Fred said, smiling now despite the seriousness of the situation.

"Thank you, Frederick. As you know, The Kid saw a British film at one point and was not used to the accent and proper diction, and hence became frightened by it."

"We're gonna need more than some snooty talk if we're gonna get this bastard," Meanie said, putting a cigar in the corner of his mouth. "Now, maybe he's getting older, and maybe he's got some creepy rag to read, but you're forgetting something, and that something is this: I have a perfect record. I have gotten to every other runt I have ever worked on, and I'll be damned if this runt is gonna break my streak."

He lit up his cigar and smoked it and chewed it at the same time, drooling mucus and snorting puffs out of his snout like some disgusting magic dragon. The others came closer, huddling around the seasoned veteran, hoping he'd offer hope for them, their mission, and their neighborhood.

"First of all," Meanie began, "we have to 'fess up to something, and I mean all three of us: We haven't been scary enough."

"Meanie!" Fred-Fred said with shock. "How could you say that?"

"That's a serious insult, sir!" Slithers agreed, indignantly hissing.

"I am saying this for your own good, and I am just as guilty of slacking off here as you guys are. We can stand around stroking ourselves, or we can face facts!"

"What facts?" Slithers demanded.

"The Kid is almost 8, Slithers. Almost 8 years old, and on top of that, he's a boy. The *boo* scares ain't gonna cut the mustard no more. If we're gonna get him, and I mean *really get him*, we have to contemporize, despite how ridiculous that seems. I know we're not used to going beyond tradition, but kids these days bring it on themselves. You know that they mock good old monsters like us! They demand more for their terror, and what kind of monsters are we if we don't provide it?"

Meanie watched as Slithers and Fred-Fred cooled their tempers, the reality of his harsh words sinking in.

"You have a solid point," Slithers admitted. "I must give you that."

"Yeah," Fred-Fred said, hating to admit it but having to.

"Now then," Meanie said, growing calmer and quieter, "I know I've been ducking out at home in the closet there, and I'll even admit that at first it was because I'd been down and out about this here mess. But lately I've been putting my head into it, and I've been cooking up a bit of a plan."

"Delectable, old chap," Slithers said, "utterly delectable."

"Whattaya have in mind, Meanie?" Fred-Fred asked.

"I think we've been too ... what you'd call impatient. We come out at night and just wanna drag that brat kicking and screaming right outta that bed of his. But when we're faced with a force field like his blankie or a bodyguard like that plush hound, we scurry back into the darkness with piss dribbling from our peters."

"But Slithers ain't got no peter," Fred-Fred said. "He's just a pile of stuff."

"Dummy up, you Underbed ninny."

"Sorry, Meanie."

"Now then, I was thinking. We gotta be more than scary, we've got to have strategy."

"What's strategy?" Fred-Fred asked, scratching with his remaining claw.

"I learned about it from reading those board games that are stacked up in my closet. All them games are about planning how you're gonna win instead of just jumping right into a shit pile and flailing around like a ding-dong. We've relied too much on just being scary. But now it ain't enough that we've got faces like a squonk and more teeth than a shark tank."

"And Slithers ain't got no face at all!"

"Fred-Fred, you ain't helping me none with that."

"Oh yeah, sorry again."

"I agree with you, Meanie," Slithers said. "We must become more cunning if we're going to get The Kid before the boogeymen come. So what sort of clever ruse did you have in mind?"

Meanie flicked the ashes off his stogie and used his cigar to point at the lump under the comforter at the foot of The Kid's bed. Sticking out from under the lump was a worn butt made of cotton, the rump of The Kid's stuffed animal protector, the intimidating doggie named Mr. Rex.

"I think I understand your train of thought," Slithers said, panting with his sock.

"We're never gonna get to that little shit with the puppy protector there," Meanie said. "I say we go for the pup."

"Aw, jeez," fretted Fred-Fred. "I dunno, guys. That dog is pretty scary."

"Well, I'll tell you what's scarier, Fred-Fred! That's the whole damn neighborhood being overrun by boogeymen! I don't want some hockey-masked killer shacking up in my closet and putting me in line to wait for some hack's job outside a *crib*, for Christ's sake! Too many monster neighborhoods have been turned into slasher slums that way. You wanna be tripping over bloody chainsaws in your own yard? You let their kind in, and soon their whole tribe will take over this joint — fairies with finger-knives, and fatsos wearing someone else's face! What kind of neighborhood would we be leaving for future generations? Call me a bigot if you want to, but I don't want no boogeys in my neighborhood, whether they're replacing me or not!"

"I know, but ..."

"But nothing! Yeah, the dog is a mean little S.O.B. I know he took your claw, Fred-Fred, I don't blame you for being afraid. He didn't take a chunk out of me, but he tore a big patch of fur outta my keister when he first took patrol in that bed. It grew back, but I ain't forgotten how I almost lost my ass to the jaws of that KB Toys Cujo!"

Fred-Fred fell silent, knowing Meanie was right. They all did, despite their growing trepidation.

"Now then," Meanie began, "I ain't gonna bullshit you guys. You're my neighbors, and more than that, you're my friends. Like you said, Slithers, we're a team. I ain't gonna stand here and tell you it will be easy to take Mr. Rex. This is an all-or-nothing deal, boys. You've gotta ask yourselves right here and now: Are we real monsters, or are we just yesterday's nightmare?"

Meanie put his cigar back into his mouth and reached forward with his fuzzy, gnarled paw. Slithers came forward with his arm, which tonight was the leg of a pair of jeans, and draped it over Meanie's fat fist. Fred-Fred saw his friend's camaraderie and knew that he had to do what was right and that even a creature under the bed had to face his own fears eventually. He came forward with his vulture-like talon and placed it on top of the other hands with a slimy *plop*.

"We are monsters!" Fred-Fred proclaimed, his eyes like glowing spirals in the darkness of The Kid's room.

"That's right," Meanie said. "And I'll tell you something else. The only thing that might replace me in that closet is this little brat's sexuality."

* * * * *

The Kid sat up, groggy but sure he'd heard the gurgling voice once again. It was the same horrible singsong that had come from beneath his mattress since he was a toddler.

"Fred-Fred, under your bed, stay tucked in or you're gonna be dead!" he heard the thing grumble.

He grabbed Mr. Rex and pulled him close to his tummy. His soft body was squishy against his face, and he liked the little hole that had formed on his back where a tiny bit of cotton fluffed out. He sucked on it now in place of his thumb. A thump came from beneath the bed, and he inhaled a small thread. It tickled his throat, preventing him from screaming. That was good. His dad had already had a long talk with him about being brave enough to sleep in his own bed. He knew he was getting too old to go crying to his parents, but he couldn't help being afraid at night. During the day he was confident, but once the deep shadows of night fell, that confidence crumbled like the toothpick house he'd made in school for Mother's Day.

Thump! Thump! Thump!

The Kid pulled his feet in close to him, far away from the edge. He knew he'd been taking a risk by untucking the blanket from the end of the bed. A mother's tuck was there for a reason. But, like his father, his feet got hot, and so he kicked them off in his sleep. That was why he placed Mr. Rex at the edge, for reinforcement. But now he was holding on to him like a semiconscious boxer holds on to the ropes, and the noise below was like a hippie drum circle gone rabid.

He dared to peek over the edge, and was immediately sorry that he had.

* * * * *

Fred-Fred knew The Kid was looking now. It was simple monster's intuition. Slithers had explained that to him. Knowing The Kid was peeking over the side, Fred-Fred had pulled back the rolls of blubber at his belly and let his tentacles unfurl. He had six of the multihued octopus limbs, and he let them flail now, three shooting out from each side of the bed, all of them hammering away like Tommy Lee on a whip-it binge.

This got The Kid going, which got the dog barking, as was Meanie's plan. Fred-Fred was excited that things were going well so far. He farted with delight and continued to pound the floorboards.

* * * * *

"Jeez," Meanie said from the dim corner. "Fred-Fred is really putting his muscle into it, huh? Full-on monster style, just like we had in the old days."

"It is a good show, good sir," Slithers said. "By now I'd say The Kid has a full helping of steamy macaroni in his britches."

"Yeah, and that fleabag doll of his is yapping up real nice. That's our cue, buddy. Let's move."

The two monsters catapulted their ghastly forms from the enveloping dark, purposefully making themselves visible in the moonlight that knifed through the wide gap in the curtains. Meanie held fast to his hobgoblin origin by doing a ghoulish jig around the bed while Slithers shimmied about and coiled up the posts of the headboard. He stuck to the end of the bed, while Meanie began to bounce around on the left, letting Fred-Fred emerge from under the right side of the mattress. This way, they surrounded the entire frame, leaving The Kid trapped and making it possible for only one of them to be assaulted by Mr. Rex. It was a toss-up, they knew, but they had a plan, and Slithers was both brave and true to his word.

Slithers had volunteered to lure the hound toward him. He knew it would be painful to be shredded to bits, but he could always re-form. If he could just tease the doggie enough with one dangling shred of his clothing carrion, it may very well give his monster teammates the edge they needed to really get The Kid once and for all. Slithers wasn't keen on potentially being mangled, but he was far less keen on the idea of living next door to some filthy boogeyman, especially if they were inspired by one of those movie remakes, the true bottom-of-the-barrel breeds. Though he considered himself an open-minded, liberal monster, he still shivered to think of the vacuous depths his property value would plummet to if boogeys started to move in. Compared to that travesty, he felt that this effort was well worth the risk of grievous bodily harm.

However, Mr. Rex went for Meanie first. He was dancing about like a horny teenager at a paint-huffing party, so the doggie rocketed to his end of the bed right away, bucking and braying like a government mule. Meanie and Slithers caught each other's eye and nodded in agreement, knowing the plan. Meanie ducked under the edge of the bed, popping his head into Fred-Fred's house. At the same time, Slithers unfurled his arm as far as it would go, ripping some of the stitching at the seam. He rolled it back up and then quickly darted it out as if snapping a towel. He cracked Mr. Rex right on his cotton-filled ass, and the doggie yelped from the pain and went spinning in the air like a pinwheel.

In addition to this, it seemed as if luck was their lady tonight, because Mr. Rex's body fell directly onto the bedpost, and its frayed edge snagged the worn hole in his back, leaving him somewhat impaled. He spun on it, spilling bits of his fluffy guts as he cried out in his failure.

Fred-Fred was first to notice the doggie's disadvantage.

"It's payback time, ya jerk!" he croaked, wrapping a tentacle around Mr. Rex's body and pulling him down farther on the post, sending the wooden pillar all the way through his back and out his belly. The doggie writhed in an agonizing death, and Fred-Fred smiled so wide at Mr. Rex's squeals of agony that he nearly dislocated his jaw.

Meanie saw what had transpired above him, and excitement pulsed in his black blood. He sprang from under the bed like an angry hornet. With the guard dog down, Meanie was so ready to attack The Kid that he completely forgot about the comforter. He raged toward the bedside, delighting at the look of abject horror that dominated The Kid's pallid face, and he slammed his paws down right on the comforter like a dumb shit. The burning sensation was like an electrical current, charring his palms and sending muscle spasms jolting through his entire body. He screamed, and so did The Kid.

Slithers was fast to react, though, and once again he whip-snapped his arm, knocking Meanie away from the dangerous comforter. But in doing so he ripped the shirt that was his upper torso, and he collapsed within himself, falling into a tangled mess upon the floor. He howled out in a muted echo as his body disappeared.

All of this commotion was enough to finally make The Kid go berserk. He began bawling huge crocodile tears and flailed about, not knowing which way to turn. He was panicking now, and in his panic he decided, stupidly, to leave the security of his bed in a desperate dash for the door. Somehow he stepped right between Fred-Fred's writhing tentacles.

Despite the fact that he was still rattled by the comforter's burning, Meanie very clearly saw The Kid making his mad dash. He wasted no time, knowing there was none left. In a thunderous somersault, he projected himself completely over the bed, forming himself into one big, blue ball of rank fur. He slammed into The Kid like a cannonball, and felt the little brat's body crumble beneath his weight as he was knocked to the floor. The Kid squirmed beneath him as he reformed, and The Kid even managed to turn over, but this brought him face to face with Meanie's mug, a hardened monster mash of a face that Meanie's own mother had deemed too ugly to kiss. The Kid squealed like a pig being branded — which, in a way, he was.

Meanie balled up his paw and slammed a hard fist into The Kid's face. His nostril expelled a hot squirt of blood, and the propulsion knocked the back of his head into the hardwood floor. Meanie let his large, brown tongue plop out of his mouth like a cat turd into the snow, steaming and stinking as it lapped up the blood from The Kid's nose. It had been so long since he'd had a taste of human gore that he'd almost forgotten how lustrous and savory it was. He let his eyes bulge out of his head to the point where the connective tissue showed, and he made his horns curve downward like a bull toward some rookie matador. Pink steam blew out of his nostrils, cloaking The Kid in a crazy haze.

"Eat him, Meanie! Eat the little bastard!" he heard Fred-Fred cheer.

Inhaling after spraying his mist, Meanie could smell the urine The Kid had let go in his pajamas. It was like a botanical garden in May to him. The little prick wasn't just shaking beneath him, he was convulsing enough to register on the Richter scale. All the blood had left his face, and the small amount of maturity that had started to blossom within The Kid had vanished now, and likely wouldn't come back for a long time.

Meanie smiled in triumph. He had made The Kid his bitch.

* * * * *

There was a brief instant of disappointment when the bedroom door was flung open. Meanie thought that the hulking shadow standing there in the hall was a boogeyman, showing up to take his place just as he was making progress. But it wasn't a new nightmare, it was just The Old Man, The Kid's pop. Meanie jumped off of The Kid and scurried back to Fred-Fred's place, wiggling under the bed frame just before the lights were flicked on.

"What in the Sam Hill are you doing in here?" The Old Man asked.

The Kid was shaking and crying on the floor in a puddle of his own piss with a trickle of blood coming out of one nostril. He was unable to control himself and jumped up at his father, wrapping his arms around him tightly.

"Son," The Old Man said, addressing him, "why are you trashing your room at eleven o'clock at night? What the heck is wrong with you?"

"They tried to eat me, Dad!" The Kid bawled.

The Old Man took a look around the room. He noticed that The Kid had broken one of his toys, the stupid dog doll that The Old Man thought he was getting too big for anyhow. He'd also apparently rolled out of bed again. It had been a long time since his bad dreams had caused him to do that, but judging by the cooling piss that pressed against his leg as his son hugged him, The Old Man figured playing soccer with some older kids wasn't growing him up as easily as he thought it might.

"They tried to eat me!" The Kid cried again. "They almost got me this time!"

The Kid pulled back his head and looked up at The Old Man. He noticed that his son had a bloody nose once again, on top of everything else. He just wouldn't stop picking. At least he wasn't eating his boogers anymore, or at least not in front of other people.

"Okay now, son," he said, patting his head and feeling a strange lump there. "Let's wash you up in the bathroom. Nobody is trying to eat you."

"But Dad …!"

"Shush!" he demanded. "Don't get your mother out of bed, you know she's pregnant and needs to rest. If she gets wind of this night terrors crap coming back, she'll want to drag you to a shrink. She's got enough to worry about with a real baby coming without having to take care of a grown boy who is acting like a baby!"

* * * * *

Under the bed, Meanie and Fred-Fred struggled to contain their laughter. The Old Man was ripping into the little brat with about as much mercy as the monsters themselves. They watched The Old Man escort The Kid out of the room to go wash his face and give him a serious talk. They looked at each other and shook hands, paw to talon.

Outside the bed, they heard Slithers reforming.

"How you doing out there, Slithers?" Meanie asked.

"I'm managing," he said. "That hurt like the dickens, but it was worth the payoff."

Slithers wiggled his way under the bed and into Fred-Fred's living room. He had rebuilt himself using a discarded sneaker, some log-cabin bits, and even some of the late Mr. Rex's cotton innards. Fred-Fred patted him on the back and tossed him and Meanie a beer each before popping open his own. He couldn't remember the last time they'd all just hung out together at his place. It felt damn good, like the neighborhood was already getting back to normal.

"I couldn't believe the way you got right in The Kid's face," Fred-Fred told Meanie. "That was gold!"

"Well, like I said before," Meanie began, "the kids these days aren't scared by the simple old ways. They need a little extra. It's more work, but that's what the market is demanding."

"Oh man," Fred-Fred said, still laughing, "when you punched him in the face! Haw-haw! I could barely breathe! I never seen anything so funny in my life!"

"Hey, you did nice work killing that mutt, too! And let's not forget Vlad the Impaler over here," he said, pointing at Slithers. "Boy oh boy, the way you smacked that mutt was beautiful!"

"It was a lucky shot, but thank you kindly," Slithers said. "And allow me to add that while I, too, enjoyed watching you punch the child, it was the licking of his blood that I saw as nothing short of artwork, my good fellow."

"You know, I really wanted to eat that brat," Meanie said, passing out cigars to go with their beers. "But you can't cut off your snout to spite your face, so to speak. This way is better. This way is the good, old-fashioned, nightmare way, and I never could have done it without you guys. You are true monsters, made of real hellfire and brimstone."

"Indubitably," Slithers agreed. "There is little chance of any boogeyman moving in on our territory now. After the horror show we put on for the boy tonight, he's bound to be frightened of us, specifically, for years to come, if not his entire life. I daresay I think we may have even secured a phobia!"

"Wow!" Fred-Fred said.

"Well, let's not get ahead of ourselves, now," Meanie said. "Maybe we did, and maybe we didn't create a phobia. Either way, I wouldn't hold your breath for no phobic bonus. But we still put in a fine night of freaking, and we should be goddamned proud of our ghoulishness."

"We got him!" Fred-Fred hollered, holding out his beer for a toast.

"Damn right," Meanie said. "We got that brat, and we got him good."

"Cheers," Slithers added, raising his beer with the jumprope that served as his new arm.

The three rusted cans clanked together in victory. The monsters had secured their neighborhood against the unwanted immigration of boogeymen. Better than that, though, they had also proven themselves, and now they would not have to worry about losing their positions, which, in their current economy, was truly something to be scared of.

The Bone Orchard

When it began, the snow was so gentle that when the wind blew, it made white wisps that danced across the wooden walkway, looking like the froth of a wild tide. But while the snow may have started gently, the wind was an ornery thing that howled in his ears, as if passing on the secret of the horror that was to come.

Cheyenne spit his tobacco and watched it begin to freeze when it hit the steps, looking like dung from a Christmas burro. He walked up the planks, mindful of the ice, and made his way into the glow of the brothel. He felt a sweet comfort the moment he stepped inside, leaving the winter flurries behind in favor of the soft lamplight that reflected off the pints of whiskey and the smell of talc that seemed to float from betwixt each pair of pearly breasts that popped out of the brims of those corsets.

Sonny's Saloon and Bordello. By gum, it'd been a while, he thought. For such a poor town, the place was mighty fine.

"Belly up to the bar, friend," the barkeep called out to him.

He wasn't in the mood to jaw with this boy, who looked between hay and grass, but his chilled bones sure could use a swish of whiskey or some good corn liquor. He'd think about sarsaparilla only if he was planning on bedding one of these harlots tonight, which he doubted. He was low on money, and he'd just as rather spend it on morphine these days than on a lady. There had been a time when he had been so regular there that he'd bedded every whore in the house. Now there were a lot of new lassies in the place, a lot of them young and firm too, but he was too broke, pissed off and old to care much.

"Just give me a snort of that oh-be-joyful, son," he told the barkeep. He reached for the cigar in his pocket, but, noting that there was only one left, he figured he'd save it for a happier occasion.

A pint of whiskey was slid his way, and he shot it down like a U.S. marshall in his angry dreams. He had taken to drinking Mule Skinners of late, over his old standby of bourbon. He felt played out, but the burn of the liquor popped his eyes open and tingled his guts afire. It wasn't the kiss of morphine, but it would do.

He scanned the place, seeing semi-familiar faces amongst the new. Mostly they were harlots, like the two blondes and the chubby brunette in the corner, but a few card players and drunks were tucked in back. Some local grangers he recognized from the old days were just leaving. The harsh winter night seemed to be bad for business. He was just wondering where Sonny himself was, when he saw him come around the side of the bar, fatter now and with a little less hair; but his eyes were the same hard, black outhouse holes they'd always been.

"This whiskey tastes like belly-wash," he snarled, grinning like a joker under the brim of his frozen hat. "I think your bar boy here is trying to bilk me with turpentine."

Sonny glared at him like an angry cock before his face softened with recognition.

"McCracken?" Sonny asked, taken aback. "Is that you, you ol' hard case?"

"The very same."

Sonny walked over to him and shook his hand. They weren't friends, exactly, but he was someone Cheyenne knew, and that was enough.

"Haven't seen you 'round these parts in some time," Sonny said, rolling up his cuffs. "I heard you were locked up in the calaboose."

"Well, when no one pays the bounty on ya, they end up sending ya right back out, if'n they don't hang ya first."

They both snickered dryly.

"Stayin' at Lady Demsy's?" he asked.

"Yeah," Cheyenne replied. He'd paid for a room for two nights, stashed his bit of plunder, and had stabled his horse in the barn Lady Demsy provided for all her tenants' steeds. His horse, Blackheart, was more of a crow-bait gelding than anything else, but being his only mode of transport and one of his only possessions, he didn't want him freezing in the night.

"Well, good to have you back, old timer," Sonny said and patted him on the shoulder before wandering off to talk with one of the girls. Cheyenne had been hoping to friendly his way into a free round, but no such luck. Sonny was the same cheap croaker he'd always been.

"Old timer," he repeated to himself.

He looked at his reflection across the bar and realized Sonny was right. He'd never seen himself look so ashen. His stubble was coming in white now, and his hair was salt and pepper at best. Even his skin had taken on a ghostly pallor, highlighting all of the old scars he'd gained in the war. Scars, a bum ankle, and a morphine habit, he thought, *and they hadn't even won*. Now he was 52 and busted.

Roaming again, just to end up back in this hellfire burg, ready to rob another railcar if he could just get a good posse off the ground.

"Another?" the barkeep asked, pointing at his empty glass.

He dug into his pocket and checked his change, glad he'd secured a room before hitting the firewater.

"I reckon one more would do me," he said.

The barkeep refilled the glass and drifted away, leaving him to guzzle his woe. But he wasn't lonesome long. No one in a whorehouse ever is.

"Howdy," she said, scooting next to him, her blond locks dancing on his shoulder. "My name's Mabel. What's yours?"

"Cheyenne McCracken," he said.

She smelled of lilac. She was young, too, and fine as cream gravy.

"Hey, isn't Cheyenne a girl's name?" she teased, as if she'd been the first one ever to do so.

"Reckon so."

"Well, you look pretty manly to me," she said, giving him the gush and batting eyes. "A real rough-and-tough cowpoke."

"Is that right?"

"Yes, indeed."

She gave him a knowing wink, and he belched in reply.

"Hell, I'm old enough to be your pappy."

"I've seen older," she said. "Besides, you've got character."

"Ain't got the money, though."

"Not even for little ol' Mabel?"

"Not even for a bath in week-old water," he told her. "Just came in to warm up."

"Well," she said, already moving away, "I'd keep you warmer than that rot-gut ever could."

As she walked off, she put a little extra swagger in her hips, driving the point home. The wind outside howled like a steam whistle, and bits of sleet began to click and clack against the windows. Cheyenne watched now as the weather turned nasty, seeing the sleet mesh with heavy flakes. They reminded him of a feathering he'd seen a preacher receive once, after the man had been slathered in tar. It was all because of a squabble over religious education in grammar schools. Looking at the snowflakes now, Cheyenne remembered the gentle float of the feathers, and how angelic it all had looked, even though they were to spell horror for the man who lay under their delicate fall.

* * * * *

"It's getting bad out there," a voice said from the top of the stairwell. It was a smoky voice he knew could not be duplicated. The sound of it was like velvet brushing across his heavy heart. It had to be her.

Looking up, he watched her walk down the steps, looking like a redheaded fairy from a children's bedtime story. Maybe it was the dim light or the heavy powder on her cheeks, or maybe the hooch was buckin' him, but from where he sat, it looked as if she hadn't aged a single season in five years. She must be close to 40 now, he realized, but she looked just as he remembered her: the same slender form and delicate, doll-like limbs, and that hair, those untamed locks of billowing sunfire. She was still a lady of the first water, he thought. He felt his mouth go dry, so he wet his lips with the last drop at the bottom of his glass.

A few of the card players got up to leave, and she tried to coax them into staying, doing her job. Two of them kept right on with their poker game, but the others just tipped their hats to her before walking out into the now-raging winter.

"This ain't no barn!" Sonny barked at them as they took too long to shuffle out. "Close the door!"

The men exited without a word, and Cheyenne figured that when you're a big bug who's got the only hot spot in a dunghill, you didn't have to give the best customer service. This was just how he remembered Sonny's disposition. Far as anyone could tell, Sonny was born an ill-mannered bastard, ready to spit into his own mama's eye.

Cheyenne only saw the outside for a split second as the front door fell back into place. But in that moment, he thought he saw something strange in the sky, beyond the showers of ice. It almost looked like something was twisting the night itself, making it churn like butter, only blacker. But the door closed, and so he just rubbed his eyes, blaming the emptied glass before him.

She was drawing closer now, much closer, even though she still had failed to recognize him under the shadow of his hat. She moved up to the bar, and even three stools away he could smell her fresh application of coumarin, which sent his mind reeling back to those hot summer nights in her arms. She said something to the barkeep and then turned his way, as if he was just another granger.

"It's getting powerful mean out there," she said. "Stormin' to the beat the Dutch. Seems a fella would be wise-minded to find a natural way to stay warm."

"That's a new flirt," he countered, the hat's brim still concealing him.

"Come on, cowpoke," she said, stepping closer. "Let Jessamine take care of you tonight."

"Jessamine now, huh?" he asked, looking up at her. "Is it all right if I just call you Mercy?"

She heard her true name just as she saw the familiarity buried within the leathery folds of his face, a face she had once kissed and truly meant it.

"Cheyenne?" she said in a hush. She sat down slowly, getting a better look at him. For a moment she didn't speak, but she reached out with one hand and touched the thick scar that ran down the right side of his face where the bayonet had nearly taken his eye.

"Cheyenne McCracken?" she asked, not believing what she saw.

"The very same," he whispered back.

She seemed as if she didn't know whether to hug him or slap him. Her eyes grew misty, and she seemed to smile and choke at the same time.

"I'd heard that you were ..."

She couldn't get it out.

"In the hoosegow?" he said.

"No. I'd heard you'd gone the way of all flesh; that you'd died fightin' for General Lee. But then I heard other scuttlebutt too, like how you was robbing banks back in the old states with a gang of copperheads."

"Well, scuttlebutt is all it was," he said. "I ain't dead, but I would be before riding with Yanks, even if they was Union-hatin'."

"Where have you been since the war?"

"Oh, you know, just between here and nowhere."

He didn't want to tell her about the railcar robberies, the shootouts, the horse tripping and the bloody duels. He didn't want to confess to the lawlessness he'd fallen right back into after the war. So there was a somber pause as they looked into each other's eyes and said nothing.

"Been gone a long time, soldier," she said.

"I reckon so."

"Anything particular bring you back here?"

He sensed some hardening of her heart, and so he tried to ease her back.

"I honestly didn't think you'd still be around, Mercy. I figured you'd moved on outta this here burg, maybe to a cottage upland. I'd heard that you were all settled down with an upstanding dude, someone to really ride the river with."

"Just a whore in a whorehouse, Cheyenne. Same as when you left, just older."

He fiddled with his glass.

"Just as I reckon you're still a gunman," she added. "Still robbing and killing and rambling like you'd just turned 18."

"I didn't realize you were so sore at me, Mercy."

She took a deep breath then, struggling in the corset.

"My apologies, Cheyenne," she said, softening. "I ain't sore at you. I'm sore at myself."

"For what?"

"For my own damned dreams."

She placed her small, freckled hands over his.

"It ain't like things ended bad between us," she said. "How could they end when they'd never really begun?"

She wasn't trying to dig at him now; this was her true heart talking, and that's what made it sting all the more. He wanted to tell her that it wasn't so, but he knew, just as she did, that there had been no courting, roses or pearls. There had been no love letters or whispered nothings. She'd been a whore and he'd been a regular customer: a lonesome local hombre who had taken a shine to her charms rather than those of the other whores he'd bedded there. A kinship had grown between them, something they both must have been desperate enough to mistake for love at the time. They'd both held on to that afterglow, neither of them knowing what it all really meant.

He sighed, wanting to tell her how he'd missed her, but it just wasn't in him to do it, just as it hadn't been in him to say goodbye. In truth, if he'd thought she still would have been there, he likely would have kept riding right through town. Not because he didn't care, but because he didn't know what to do with that caring. He had heard that she'd left Sonny's. He'd heard she had married and had a flock of little ones, and for her sake he had hoped it was true. But so much for what he'd heard.

To his surprise, she got off of her stool and leaned in to kiss his cheek.

"Good to see you, though, anyway," she said, sweetly.

That's when the window exploded.

* * * * *

Ice rained in like a hail of bullets, mixing with the broken glass to make a hellish spray. It was the rear window of the saloon that had somehow burst, and now the snow came hammering in. The glass and ice had discharged across the card players in the back of the house. Both of them had fallen to the floor, upending the table and sending their aces and kings adrift in the wind.

"Tarnation!" one of them hollered as he got to his knees. He was stout and portly, so it took him a moment to stand. His buddy, however, remained still on the floor, an icicle the size of a sabre having pierced his throat.

Mercy had run to the poor man's side before Cheyenne had even gotten off his stool. He approached everything gingerly these days, after all he'd seen as a soldier and a bandit. Sonny had gone to the window, trying to assess the damage, and the barkeep stood there gawking, as did Mabel, terrified by the blood pooling around the dead man's gushing neck. The two other whores in the back remained locked in place, breathlessly watching.

"We need to get Doc Wilford over here, right away!" Mercy cried.

"Zeke?" the portly card player called out to his buddy. "Oh no, Zeke!"

They gathered around him and stood there for a moment, staring, lost.

"We should get him outside," Sonny said, all matter-of-fact.

"Outside?" Mercy said. "Are you crazy, Sonny? He needs medical care, and you want to toss him out in the storm?"

"Look at him!" Sonny said, pointing. " He's dead! All he's gonna do in here now is bleed all over my floor!"

"You cold-hearted bastard!" the card player shouted.

"Hobble your lip, Rufus!" he replied. "I've gone through the mill enough to know a corpse when I see one."

Rufus' face turned red, and he glowered at Sonny but didn't reply. He just turned back to Zeke and then crouched by his side with Mercy.

"We should get the doc, Sonny," she said. "Zeke here might still be alive."

Cheyenne had made it over to them now, and, looking down at poor Zeke with the frozen stake through his Adam's apple, he knew that Sonny was right. Zeke was stone dead. But that didn't detract from Mercy's Christian intentions. Her true name suited her, he thought.

"Stop fussin' over him, and fetch the mop," Sonny barked at her. "I don't want his blood to stain."

Cheyenne turned to Sonny, about to tell him to pull in his horns and mind his tone, but he was distracted by what he saw behind Sonny, out there in the darkness behind the broken window. He moved past the others to the sill, feeling the snow biting at his face. He peered into the backyard of the brothel, looking past the storm that tried its best to cloak the movement of the shadowy figures within it. But he saw them anyway, twisting out there in the white banks like circus geeks. They were black, spindly things that sprang from the murk only to peter out of sight, camouflaged by the contrast of the darkness against all that blinding white. It was as if the night sky was coughing up critters, only to inhale them once again, sending the flailing slivers back into the blackness.

But the night sky itself was even stranger. On the horizon, the sky seemed to pulsate and spin, as if the night were made of oil, churning as the storm intensified. It throbbed as if it had its own heartbeat, pumping rapidly and bubbling up. And as he looked closer, he realized that this cyclone was actually inverted and imploding like a dynamited mine. And just as his eyes could adjust to it, they lost focus, and all he could see was starless night and snow. But if he kept looking, it revealed itself again and again before vanishing.

"What are you doing just standing there, McCracken?" Sonny said.

"There's something out there," he said.

"I know, the storm of the year. Now move aside so I can board it up!"

Sonny walked over to a small closet and retrieved some planks. He spun back around, holding the nails in his lips and a hammer in his fist. The barkeep came over and helped him.

"He really is dead," Mercy said, still at Zeke's side.

Mabel had gone and grabbed the mop for her, and was trying to clean up the mess, while Rufus remained crouched there, thunderstruck. His handlebar moustache quivered as he fought back tears. Cheyenne tried to get a better look at the cyclone and the things he saw slithering in and out of it, but an arctic gust blew in, hitting him with a wall of white. He stumbled back, stunned by the intensity of the cold air. Even up in New England, he had never felt anything so chilling.

"Gosh," Mabel said, shaking. "It must be 10 below out there!"

She gathered the broken glass with her long fingernails and plopped the pieces into a bucket while Sonny and the barkeep began boarding up the hole. Sonny turned and looked at Zeke's body with a snarl.

"Somebody had better go fetch the sheriff," he said. "Better he see that icicle in Zeke's neck before the evidence melts and we have to convince him that this here wasn't no knife fight over them cards."

Sonny turned to the barkeep, hinting with his iron stare.

"Aw, Sonny," he complained. "The sheriff's station is at the edge of town!"

"I don't care a continental. Now go on, get a wiggle on!"

"But I could freeze to death."

"You could also starve to death if you lose your job, boy, you and that sickly mother of yours," Sonny snapped. "Now if you wanna keep on as my barkeep, you's best do as I tell ya."

Cheyenne watched the barkeep gulp before walking over to the rack to grab his coat. Mercy stood up, a look of bewilderment on her pale and pretty face.

"Please, you can't send him out in this, Sonny," she argued. "We don't need the sheriff right off. We can fetch him come morning. We have enough witnesses here to explain what happened."

"Hogwash," he said. "That lousy sheriff would love to get the upper hand on me, get a few free rides outta you ladies for his deputies and then drink up on my dime. He won't listen to witnesses like y'all. The word of a gaggle of whores, a drunken gambler, and a shootist ain't gonna come to much."

Mercy turned away from him and walked over to the corner where two of the other prostitutes, Eva and Nelly, stood watching in silent obedience. She looked to them, and when they caught her glance they lowered their heads in shame. They weren't about to back her up. Not to Sonny.

"Why am I not surprised?" Mercy hissed at them.

The barkeep reached the door and Nelly walked over to him. She was a blond girl of only 19, still sweet and gullible, even though her profession had matured her quite a bit over the past 14 months. She grabbed his hat off the hanger at the door and handed it to him, almost as if in apology.

"Stay warm," she said.

He nodded to her and opened the door. She stepped back, but not enough, having not expected the slender, black arms to come reaching for her. Through the gap in the doorway they came ripping — two slick limbs with long, bony fingers. They grabbed at Nelly with the ferocity of wild dogs, tearing at her dress and tugging her down to the floor by her hair. She fell so quickly that no one had time to reach her before a second pair of tar hands came stretching out of the storm. Together the hands all pulled at her, and she screamed as the exposed skin of her shoulders began to freeze and crack against their touch. One of the hands muted her then by slamming down onto her mouth, and her face began to bubble up with instant frostbite, the blisters popping apart in bursts of blood.

With a single lunge, they pulled her away into the cold night.

The barkeep took a few steps backward before collapsing in a near faint. Eva had turned to Mercy by now, burying her face in her neck. Mercy could only hold her while they both cried out in horror.

Cheyenne was the one to act. He ran to the doorway and went to slam it shut, but before he could, the shock hit him. Outside he saw the blackness that was stretched out before him in a blank eternity. The post office across the street was no longer there. The blacksmith's shop and the train station were gone. The town of White Willow was no more. There was nothing beyond the front step of the brothel except the raging ice storm and this seemingly endless chasm of black sludge.

"My God," he muttered.

In the center of the vortex, he saw Nelly's now-skeletal face as she sank into the nothingness. She reached out to him with an arm that shattered off of her shoulder as she shrieked, the little shadowy things pulling her deeper into their cyclone.

Their laughter sounded almost childlike as he slammed the door.

* * * * *

"What's going on here?" Rufus hollered, his tears now let loose.

"Nelly," Mabel cried, trembling from what she'd seen. "Oh, dear Nelly."

Cheyenne had his hand on his belt, itching toward his Colt revolver even though there was nothing to shoot at. He felt Mercy's presence behind him. She was shaking. He turned to face her, not knowing what to say or do, or even what to think.

"What is it, Cheyenne?" she whispered with panic in her eyes. "What in the name of God is it?"

He thought it over for a second.

"Darkness," he replied.

He pulled her into the nook of his arm and held her as she cried softly. Cheyenne noticed that the barkeep had gotten to his feet and was staring out the window.

"You see it too, boy?" Cheyenne asked him.

He nodded.

"At least I know I ain't crazy, then."

"But what the hell is it?" the barkeep asked.

"Don't know, but I wouldn't be standing too close to them windows if I was you."

He backed up, but not much, hypnotized by the unreal reality outside. Sonny went to his side and glanced out at it. Confusion and fear turned to anger in the saloon owner's face, and he waved his hand at the murk.

"Bosh!" Sonny said. "It's just some kind of tornado or something."

"You ignorant old whip!" Mercy said.

"Watch your tongue, missy!"

"You ever see a tornado made out of black slime?" Cheyenne asked him. "Look out there, Sonny. Everything's gone. All of White Willow, gone up the flume! Ain't nothin' out there but darkness!"

"Well, where did it come from, McCracken? And what the hell does it want with us?"

"What do *they* want with us?" Eva said.

Cheyenne turned to her. She was a buxom brunette with sad, dark eyes. She moved out of the corner now, staring right at him as she did so.

"Those things that grabbed Nelly," she said. "What were they?"

"I ain't certain. I only saw the arms."

"But you saw them at the back window, didn't you? I heard you say there was something out there."

All eyes fell upon him now.

"Yeah, I thought I saw something out there in the backyard, where the bank rises below that tree."

Cheyenne noticed the odd way that Eva and Mercy exchanged glances then as he pointed to the yard behind the saloon.

"Out back?" Mabel asked from behind him. "In the yard?"

He turned and saw how her face had fallen so white that even her rouge couldn't disguise it. Her eyes grew watery and darted about in her little skull.

"Looked like," he said. "Why? What's in the yard?"

"Nothing, that's what," Sonny said, too quickly.

Cheyenne ignored him and turned to Mercy instead.

"What is it?" he asked. "Why'd y'all get weird on me when I mentioned the backyard?"

"Because …"

"Hobble your lip, Mercy!" Sonny yelled.

Cheyenne moved quickly, slugging Sonny right in his gut. The wind escaped him and he curled over, dropping his remaining boards and the hammer. Cheyenne placed his boot heel on Sonny's shoulder and knocked him onto his back.

"Don't interrupt!" Cheyenne told him.

He turned back to Mercy, noting how her eyes had changed and the small curl at the corner of her lips. It was almost how she used to look at him in the deep hours of their shared nights, when she would tell him things she didn't tell anyone else.

"Go on," he said.

"Cheyenne," she said. "Well, we don't call it the backyard. We call it the bone orchard."

Sonny didn't have to interrupt her this time. Mabel did, by screaming.

* * * * *

It was like a geyser of pure molasses.

The boards at Mabel's feet splintered and cracked, and the sludge shot up all around her in an instant. It had come up through the floor. The tar formed ropes that sprang up her bustle and coiled about her legs. It burned coldly through her stockings and then froze to her skin, securing a solid hold as more climbed the nuances of her flesh. An upward burst of snow decorated her flailing body, and she reached out to the others as she was devoured by the murk.

"Help me!" she sobbed.

Mercy tried to run to her, but Cheyenne scooped her up with one arm and clutched her to him.

"Ain't nothing you can do for her," he whispered in her ear. "Don't let that stuff get on ya, too."

The others seemed to know it was best to stay back, or else they were paralyzed by fear, especially when the pooling tar began to bulge and change shape, the end of the ropes turning into little hands that began to drag Mabel down. Rising up from between those hands came oil-slicked skulls, followed by shoulders and tiny torsos. It was as if the slime was birthing toddlers to do its horrible bidding. Cheyenne watched them twist into life, hearing their small bones pop into existence as they slithered up Mabel's body, coating her in black ice. Even as she opened her mouth for a final scream, icicles formed between her lips, burying her final cry.

One of the oily midgets jumped upon her back and sent its claws into her shoulders. Cheyenne saw some of its malformed face now. The slime was slowly falling away from its head, revealing a pink layer of flesh so thin that he could see the thing's veins pulsing underneath. It was the last thing he saw before Mabel was pulled under the black pool and was gone forever.

The barkeep ran for the door that led to the backyard. Cheyenne threw out a leg and tripped the boy, then kicked him over when he hit the floor. The barkeep tried to get up and lash at him, but he secured his boot over the boy's throat.

"Don't go fussin', son," he said.

"We must get out of here!"

"Ain't nowhere to go to. You saw outside. If you open that door, you won't be letting us out, you'll be letting them in."

"They're already getting in!" he cried. "We're sitting ducks here! If we don't make a break, we'll be dead!"

"Nothing's out there but the ice, the tar, and those things. Best we can do is hunker down."

"Until what?" Mercy asked.

He stood there, unable to answer her.

"We ain't safe in here, Cheyenne," she said.

"Don't open the door!" Eva said.

She came to Cheyenne's side and clutched his arm. Her eyes were frantic, and her makeup was running with her tears.

"They're coming for us," she told him. "Just like Verdie swore. When she left, she swore she'd get the vex on this place!"

"Who's Verdie?"

With that, Sonny intervened.

"Enough, Eva!" he said. "Don't be playing to the gallery now with no tall tales."

Cheyenne had already given him the fist, so now he drew his coattail back to show Sonny his colt, letting him know that it would be next.

"Look, McCracken," Sonny said. "Just because you're heeled don't give you no authority. I am the proprietor of this here establishment, and I can fetch my shotgun right quick!"

"So fetch it," Cheyenne challenged.

"A curly wolf like you would just shoot me in the back!"

"No, I'll wait here like a thoroughbred," he said. "I wont even fill my hand till you've got both of yours wrapped around that peacemaker of yours."

Sonny just looked at him, debating it for a moment.

"Pony up and fetch it," Cheyenne told him.

But he didn't. He moved slowly to a stool and sat, silenced now.

Rufus saw that Cheyenne and Sonny were distracted with each other, and he took this opportunity to take Eva by the throat and put his repeater pistol to her temple. When she tried to scream, he choked her, and she squeaked like a frightened rat. The others turned around then as Rufus dragged her back a few steps, away from the group.

"None of y'all move!" he yelled.

"Rufus, no!" Mercy begged him.

"Let the lady go," Cheyenne advised him. His coattail still hung back and his fingers wiggled now on his holster.

"They want them!" Rufus said. "Don't you see? They want the women! They're the ones they keep coming for, so why don't we just give them up?"

"You lowly son of a bitch," Mercy said. It was the first time any of them had ever heard her swear.

"Let her go," Cheyenne said again.

"They're just whores!" Rufus said, dragging her closer to the back door. "Why should we all wait around to die when we can just offer up what these things want?"

"You're gonna die directly if you don't let her go, hoss."

Cheyenne's hand cupped his holster and, seeing it, Rufus panicked. He pulled his pistol away from Eva and spun it toward Cheyenne. It was all the time Cheyenne needed to draw, aim, and fire.

The back of Rufus's head came apart like a tossed watermelon, and a hot spray splattered the door behind him as he fell toward it. He'd been gripping Eva's throat so hard that he continued to do so as he rattled into death, dragging her backward with him. The two of them smashed into the back door, knocking it open, letting an ill wind come inside, followed by the small, shadowy forms that leapt like hungry wolverines from the white mounds.

Cheyenne opened fire on the creatures as they went for Eva. Tar encompassed the doorframe as the snow whirled before them in a disorienting haze. But still he fired at them, his bullets swallowed by the swirling gunk of their bodies, seeming not to faze them. In a moment they had entangled Eva in tendrils that had sprung from their bellies. Cheyenne saw that there were more of them now, about nine. Each of them had lost some of their black coating, and their freakish, translucent skin shone pink against the snow. The long worms that grew out of their stomachs had each grabbed a limb of Eva's body, and the final worm wrapped around her neck.

With the strength of a dozen horses, they quartered her.

Behind him, he heard Mercy scream as she watched her friend be ripped apart. The others watched in shocked disbelief, their horror too great to express. Cheyenne, void of other ideas, ran toward the door, letting his Colt do the talking for him. The bullets ripped through the frigid air and hit their targets with a squish. Even at closer range they seemed to have no effect. He watched them separate Eva's body and then scatter about the piles of snow, as playful as kittens with yarn; all except the one who held her decapitated head in its hands, lapping at the gushing stump.

Cheyenne had expected to see the face of a horrible beast. He'd expected a godless thing with a bull's grimace and a demon's burning eyes. Having seen a monster of the highest order, he'd thought there would be a face to match. What he did not expect to see was a familiar face, the most familiar face possible. It was the same youthful smirk that had greeted him in the mirror when he was a just a little boy.

* * * * *

For the first time in over thirty years, Cheyenne recited the Lord's Prayer.

My face, he thought. *That thing had my face, my face from when I was just a wee child.*

He'd never felt such fear. Not in battles, showdowns, or duels.

The little creature had looked up at him with his own eyes and then bent its head back down to suckle at Eva's bloody neck. As it had buried its head, red hair began to sprout from its albino skull, growing fuller with each slurp it took. Then, as another gush of snow had blown in and hammered at Cheyenne, the creature shrank away with the head in its paws, smiling at Cheyenne instead of attacking him.

It wants me to see, he thought. *It wants me to understand.*

And in return, he wanted to.

Despite the fear that made him shake, the curiosity was strong, and stronger still was the pull. It was like he'd been lassoed. Something was hauling him farther out into the blizzard. It was beckoning him like a siren's song carried on the wind, the howl like an old train pulverizing the rails. He moved slowly through the knee-high snow, shuffling in a trance until he came upon it.

Below the withered sycamore where the valley opened, the snow bank gave way to a clearing. The icicles on the dead tree's branches worked like compass needles, directing him toward the ground. The wind pushed at the snow, and it gave way gently, dissipating into the night to reveal the little pits in the hollow.

Cheyenne looked down at the nine unearthed graves before him.

He bent down on one knee and stared into them. Reaching into one, he brushed away the dirt that covered the small shape within. Bracing the fragile form with his palm, he pulled it up, it being small enough to support with just one of his hands. He used the other to brush the remaining dust away from the skeletal form.

Cheyenne realize that he had stopped breathing, so he forced himself to take a deep breath. The air felt thick and colder than death itself.

He placed the infant's skeleton back in its shallow grave and looked into the other eight holes. He was not surprised by what he found in them.

When he made it back to the brothel, he stood in the doorway and saw Mercy standing there with great tears blurring her eyes. Her hands were clutched over her heart.

"Tell me of the bone orchard," he said.

* * * * *

"We've all always tried to prevent it," Mercy explained as she sat there at the bar, nervously fiddling with her wet handkerchief. "It isn't easy to get our customers to just … pull out … you know. They pay good money, and they want to have a good time."

Cheyenne was waiting for Sonny to interject, but now he was sullen and quiet, sitting there on the stool with his head down.

"But we do try to prevent it," Mercy said, sniffling. "We've got sponges with carbolic acid and quinine, but in a pinch we use lemon juice. Lately some of us have been using these new beeswax caps we got. But the contraceptives are up to us. Can't ask no paying cowboy to put on a rubber sheath."

She looked up at Cheyenne, but he said nothing.

"Sonny keeps us in these corsets," Mercy continued. "They ain't just to make us attractive to the costumers, either. If one of us gets in a family way, these corsets can hide it, as well as help to … remove the … obstruction."

"You mean …?" Cheyenne asked.

"Miscarriages," she said. "Ain't nobody got use for no pregnant whore. Once one of us started to go through the quickening, feeling the baby move, we had to do what we could to remove the … unwanted obstruction. Sonny had all kinds of cures to keep us working and to prevent having another mouth to feed."

"Like what?" Cheyenne asked, looking hard at Sonny.

"Can't afford no doctors, you know," Mercy explained, crying. "We'd never know we was pregnant until we felt the baby kick."

"What cures did you have, Sonny?" Cheyenne asked him directly.

"Look, McCracken," Sonny said, "a baby ain't like a child. A child can be put to work and earn their keep. This is a whorehouse! Ladies on their backs all day pleasing men are bound to get a blockage of their monthly now and then. So we did what we had to do."

"He'd work us harder," Mercy said. "Any of us ladies who were going through the quickening would get the heavy chores and longer hours on horseback. That would take care of things a lot of the time. If that failed, there was always ergot, quinine and purgatives. I will not shame myself by detailing their usage."

She dabbed at her tears and Cheyenne stepped closer to Sonny.

"And what of the ones you couldn't get rid of?" he asked. "What of them?"

Sonny kept staring at the floor, so Cheyenne shoved him.

"What of them, Sonny? What of the unwanted born?"

But Sonny had turned to stone, his lip buttoned for once.

Next to him, sitting on the floor with his knees pulled to his chest, was the barkeep. He'd had his face buried in his crossed arms, but now Cheyenne could hear his soft sobbing. He walked over and stood before him. The kid looked up, his face wet and pink and guilty.

"My mother is a lunger," he said. "She has the consumption."

Cheyenne watched him cry and waited.

"I need this job. I have to do what Sonny tells me, mister," he pleaded. "I didn't want to hurt them babies. He told me it was the best thing we could do. Better than deserting them in this mean ol' world."

Cheyenne felt something harden in his chest.

"Tell me," he said.

"Nine of them; nine in six years. Sonny wouldn't get no midwife. The ladies would birth them, and then he'd pass them on to me. He told me they were used to water and darkness from being in their mamas' bellies. We have an old barrel out back that catches rain ..."

The barkeep began to sob again, unable to finish his confession, but he didn't have to.

"Like dogs," Cheyenne said. "Drowned 'em like little goddamned dogs."

They all hung their heads now, the guilt weighing them down like chains. Cheyenne looked out through the cracks in the boarded window. The snow had piled up to the sill now and was falling in. In the darkness beyond, nine faces glowed. They were still out there, waiting.

He moved over to Mercy and took her hand in his. He placed his hand beneath her chin, trying to get her to look up at him. She refused, turning away, crying.

"I know now why you were so sore at me for leaving," he said. "I left you with child, didn't I?"

Her hair fell in front of her like a curtain, her shoulders heaving as she sobbed.

"Tell me the truth, Mercy."

She took a deep breath, and then she did.

"I hid it for nine months, Cheyenne. I hid him until I could hide him no more. Nearly died giving birth to him on my own in the barn. When I came out of the coma, he was already gone. Gone to the bone orchard."

The room fell into complete silence. The boards of the building stopped creaking. Even the wind outside went mute. He stared at her for a good long while, watching the grief explode through her like an electric shock. He felt the tears fill his eyes, though they did not fall. He stared at her for a long time before turning to Sonny.

"It was just another whorehouse baby," Sonny pleaded.

Cheyenne unsheathed the Colt.

"It was the only sensible thing to do," Sonny said.

Cheyenne knew that he had only one bullet left. He knew he should be careful not to waste it. He aimed at Sonny's gut and fired. He enjoyed watching his body jerk as pain ripped through him. A gut shot was only proper, he thought. It would hurt more, and the bastard would die slow. Sonny winced and gnashed his teeth as blood began to fill his hands, but his eyes stayed open, staring out into the nothingness beyond the window.

"Vexed by a whore," Sonny said with a bitter laugh. "Verdie swore she'd put the voodoo on me when she woke to find I'd drowned her twins. How was I to know she wanted to keep them babies and give up on whoring?"

He coughed up blood and twitched a bit.

"Should have known Verdie was Simon pure with that voodoo stuff," he said. "Came up here from New Orleans."

He laughed sardonically between bloody teeth.

"Vexed by a whore," he said again. "Up the stout by a gypsy whore."

"Not yet, Sonny," Cheyenne told him. "You don't get to die yet."

* * * * *

With the back door open, the barroom quickly began to ice over. Snow flew in with blizzard strength and blanketed everything in white powder, while the temperature formed new frost.

Cheyenne dragged Sonny out by his collar. He was still alive but too weak to resist. He didn't even argue. Then Cheyenne went around the other side of the bar and fetched Sonny's double-barrel peacemaker. He had expected more of a fight from the barkeep, but the kid was still in a strange state of shock. When Cheyenne ordered him up, he did as he was told, and Cheyenne had no trouble marching him out the back door.

They stood in the pounding snow over Sonny. Cheyenne noticed that his blood was turning into red ice. He put the shotgun into the small of the kid's back.

"Pick up your boss, boy."

The barkeep lifted Sonny in his arms, cradling him. Expanding before them was the blackness, surging into infinity. But the valley remained, ending at the hollow where the dead sycamore drooped.

"Take him to the bone orchard," Cheyenne said, and the barkeep began to walk.

When they reached the shallow graves, Cheyenne saw that they were brewing with black tar. It seeped out and bubbled like lava. The blackness was consuming everything now, turning everything into an endless, churning oblivion.

They rose from the molasses like vapor, forming again out of nothing. Their umbilical cords lashed out like whips, wrapping around Sonny and the barkeep. They pulled them closer and encompassed them both in their freezing tar limbs. Sonny's bloody ice began to cover his body like a giant scab, coating the barkeep's arms that held him. Cheyenne stepped back as he heard them both begin to scream.

Rapid frostbite overcame them, and Cheyenne watched as their bodies bruised and cracked away. Their noses fell in oily drops, their limbs broke away like autumn leaves, and their mouths overflowed with black water that froze solid in their throats. The barkeep collapsed as his spine snapped in half, and his legs shattered like porcelain as he hit the ground. Sonny's remains tumbled forward and stuck in the crude of the graves. The unwanted shadow children gathered around him and the barkeep, and began to feed.

Cheyenne could see their faces now. One looked like Mabel, another like Nelly. Two of them looked like Eva. There was a set of twins as well, tiny and ghoulish. His boy was there too, his familiar face buried in the barkeep's stomach, so that all Cheyenne could see of him was Mercy's red hair.

He heard footfalls in the snow behind him, and he turned.

Mercy had left the saloon, which was just as well. The blackness had begun to consume it. The roof was gone already, and the walls were dripping as the old whorehouse was devoured by the night. She seemed to drift forward like a lovely ghost. When she reached him, he saw that her tears had frozen to her rosy cheeks. She leaned forward and kissed him goodbye.

When he opened his eyes again, he saw that the children had surrounded them.

His boy had taken his mama's hand now, and black ice was already climbing up to her elbow.

"Don't, Mercy," he said.

"I have to," she said. "I feel it in my heart, Cheyenne. I belong with them in this purgatory."

"You're not responsible for what happened, Mercy. You tried to keep him."

"But I knew about the bone orchard. I knew what was happening to the unwanted. I turned my head, Cheyenne. Turned my head while they drowned babies in potato sacks. We all knew, and we all let it go on."

Her face began to blister as the snow grew dark around them.

He wanted to turn it all back somehow, and make them young enough again to feel what they had felt before. He wanted to right the wrong of his leaving. But he could see in her face that there was no chance of happiness for Mercy now. There was simply no coming back from the guilt and sorrow that now led her into the chasm.

They took her gently into the falling snow, the vortex opening like a new wound. Cold shadows embraced her, and he looked on helplessly as she disintegrated into the void. The last thing he saw was a few strands of red hair dancing on the slope of one pale, freckled shoulder, and then it too was gone.

Cheyenne fell to his knees there in the hollow. It was all that remained. The whorehouse was gone, as was all of White Willow. Even the sycamore had vanished into the black. There was only this small patch of snow-covered valley. He was alone within it beneath the raging cyclone, until they came to join him.

He looked up at his boy's gray face.

"I know," Cheyenne told him, nodding. "I know, son."

He felt his tears leave his eyes at last.

"I wasn't wanted either," he said. "Mama wasn't no whore, just promiscuous, I guess you'd say. Daddy was a mean old hard case. Beat and whipped me, and worked me like a mule before he ran off. Mama wanted a girl, see, a little princess to name Cheyenne. Even when I was born a boy, she kept on with that."

The snow fell down into his hands as they began to crack and bleed.

"She tried to sell me after Daddy ran off," he said. "But I was malnourished and weak. No good for laboring. So when she realized she couldn't sell me, she left me at a railway. She told me to stay put, that she was going to fetch us some cornpone. But she just hopped a train and never looked back."

He felt his lips chapping and his feet going numb.

"My own mother done gave me the mitten," he said. "Couldn't find shelter no place, neither. Not even at the gospel mill. That's how I started into stealing, then robbing."

He looked up at them, but the snow blindness was making them fade away.

"I know, son," he said. "I know what it is to be unwanted. The only time I was wanted was on a sheriff's poster."

He huddled inward and collapsed. On the ground, he saw their feet backing away.

"I'm ready to stand the gaff," he said. "I've been hellbound for a bone orchard of my own anyway."

He closed his eyes, ready for them to shred him apart and pull him into that terrible nothingness. But all he felt was the chill of the snow as it continued to float down, covering him in a chilling veil.

* * * * *

Cheyenne awoke with a gasp that hurt his lungs.

He sat up and let the snow fall off his chest. He blinked the frost from his eyes and gazed into the piercing blue sky. From behind one solitary cloud, the sun shot down Jacob's ladders of golden light that shone upon the valley.

The graves behind him had been repacked with dirt.

He slowly got to his feet and looked past the whorehouse to the town of White Willow. It was snowbound but all there. A carriage went by in the slush, and a few shop patrons dodged its spray as they moved on.

He began to walk up the embankment, noticing the bits of black ice that were still melting away, the final traces of the nothingness. The doorway to the back of the saloon still had some of the tar clinging to it, but he figured that it too would soon vanish. Inside, all of the bodies were now gone, and he paid little attention to the blood that caked the walls. He just went to the bottles at the bar and upended the entire stock, giving himself a swig of the bourbon before he dumped the rest across the counter. He took his one remaining stogie from his pocket, and then his box of matches. He lit up the cigar, and then lit up Sonny's whorehouse.

He walked out into the street as Sonny's began to billow smoke. The warmth of the fire felt good, but he wanted to get out of the shade, so he left the porch. The sun was full in the sky now, having moved away from that last lingering cloud. Even on this winter morning, he could feel its generous warmth. He walked with his face turned upward, smiling at the light. He basked in it, enjoying the sunshine now on behalf of all the unwanted that never could.

Soon There'll Be Leaves

I'd decided that I wanted to die of a heart attack.

I was alone in Ron's beaten Chevy Malibu that I'd borrowed — sitting there amongst his pawnshop CDs 'n' fast-food wrappers, just fermentin' there in the parkin' lot of the hospital and bakin' in the sun. Mama was in that hospital, dyin' — fallin' apart like a swing set in the rain. At that moment she was having her dialysis done. Between all them treatments, it was hard to get any time with her 't all — and even when I did, she was doped up, overtired, or vomiting.

I decided that a fatal heart attack was the way to go for me.

Awful as it may be, it would be quick. Your life would just end, I s'pose. All that was *you* would go: hopes, dreams, and memories — your damned everythin'. Gone in the flick of a Bic. The downside of modern medicine is that it can really drag out a dyin'. Some people think it's better to have time to accept death and deal with the many emotional stages that it comes with. But as I sat in that rusty turd, I couldn't think of anythin' more horrible than to milk a death. It was like the tearin' off of a bandage.

Just rip it off, don't make me feel every individual hair as it's plucked. Please, God, have mercy.

With death, more time didn't bring peace — it just brought more sufferin'. For the dyin', it was more time spent fallin' apart, more pain, and more forfeited dignity. For the loved ones, it was more knotted stomachs as you stressed every time the phone rang, fearin' the worst. *Just rip that bandage off,* I thought. *Lord, don't let me wither in no hospital bed with cranky nurses in pajamas all talkin' to me like a boogered child while they empty out my crap bag. Just let me be there a moment, and then gone the next.*

Easy.

Please, Jesus, if I gotta die, gimme a heart attack before you gimme cancer.

I sat just watchin' the sunny nothin'. It was snowin' in New Hampshire when I'd left just a few days prior, but this was Florida — swamp country. The air had weight to it, too — it made you feel like you were shufflin' through a cloud of piss. The place had never seemed a suitable habitat for people, if you were to ask me. But most folks don't ask much of an ex-con meat cutter, and I can't say that I blame 'em.

I cursed the brightness and closed my eyes for a moment. I daydreamed, then, of being in a backyard I didn't have, choppin' logs made of the fallen trees. I fantasized of the wife I also didn't have watchin' me hack wood with an ax, only to see me kilt over, clutchin' at my chest. I thought of her running to my dead side with big ol' tears bursting from her cheeks. I liked the idea and made an oath to eat more salty meats.

It was almost 10:30. I'd been up since 5 and still hadn't eaten. It was too early for a beer or something stronger, but already I was lookin' forward to drownin' myself with a few and driftin' into the gentle numbness that soothed my heart a little. To paraphrase David Allan Coe, *I needed to renew my friendship with Jim Beam.* Still, I thought it'd be good to get some breakfast in me first, like a mornin' taco or a nice road sausage. In some places it was easy to find family-run cafes that served all kinds of good fixin's. But I was back in my old hometown of Melbourne, the soggy and diseased hole of Central Florida, so I'd soon be settling for the very kind of road sustenance that my old friend Ron ate on a regular basis, judging by the floor of the Malibu.

Mom would be getting her treatment for hours, and then she'd be asleep after that. I'd basically come all the way down again to see her for 20-minute intervals, so now I started the car and some bad pop-country music leaked through the cracked speakers on the dash. *Damn, Johnny Cash is cool again, but they still play these all-hat-and-no-cattle posers instead. I reckon part of gettin' old is hatin' new music.* I pulled out of the lot and went searchin' for anywhere with a lit Boar's Head sign.

To my disgust, I started thinkin' about Helen again.

I'd broken up with her nearly a month ago, and I was still playin' repeats of our arguments in my skull — like watchin' sitcom reruns on a borin' afternoon. Her madness and manipulations made for rather memorable miseries, and I found that my headspace had become a minefield of 'em. But even in my current state of heartache with Mama, I didn't reach out to Helen. I didn't return her late-night calls or nothin'. I wouldn't give her the satisfaction of consolin' me, because I knew that her Florence Nightingale act was just something she'd later hold over my head or even mock me for. I also knew that nothin' made a woman claw the walls like bein' ignored, and after the needless aneurism that she'd made of whatever the Hell we were, I figured I owed her nothin' but the best in complete disinterest.

It's a cowboy thang.

Her late-night messages ranged from breathy angel to frothin' buck.

"I just want to know that you're doing okay," she said in Monday's voicemail. "Even if you don't care about me anymore, you should understand that I care about you. If situations were reversed, you'd be checking on me too."

But Tuesday night it was her snide caw, sayin': "Fine, Bill. Don't even have the decency to call me back, like a gentleman would have. Like a *real man* would have. Fuck it all, it doesn't matter anyway, does it? Because you fucking left, just like you always do. Just run away from everything, little boy."

I deleted her message on Wednesday without even listenin' to it. Toleratin' 'em was too much like being back with her: moments of warmth suddenly ruined by her broken personality, leavin' me with nothin' but confusing anxiety and directionless rage. That was Helen — a beautiful sex addict with a great sense of humor one minute, and a scratched record of motiveless bitchiness the next. She'd told me once that she'd been in and outta therapy for a mood disorder, but she never stuck to the meds all them shrinks had tried to give her. Havin' been forced to see plenty of shrinks myself to get my own issues under some control, I knew she needed more help than she could ever admit to herself.

After passing abandoned strip malls that were slathered with graffiti and big ol' "space for rent" banners, I figured that a grocery store would be my best bet for breakfast, so I pulled into the parkin' lot of the Publix.

As I did, my cell began to hum. I feared it was the hospital first, always did. Then I thought it might be another rant or love poem from Helen, dependin' on the coin toss of her heart. But when I pulled it from my belt, I saw that I had a text. I never sent these things, but I got them sometimes from people. I'd only recently learned how to even check them on the damned phone. I hit the button and saw the brief message: "Heard you're back in town. Would LOVE to see you. Could be lots of fun, babe. Xxx."

There was a winkin' smiley face at the end of it — the type of inane crap that people should really stop doing once they hit puberty. My phone identified the caller as someone who'd had my new number for about two weeks, even though I'd known her many years ago, in the bad old days.

Whitney. For Christ's sake, it was a flirty text from Whitney.

* * * * *

After years of refusin' to have one due to my lack of interest in technology and even other folks, Helen had finally managed to get me onto one of them social-networkin' web pages. She'd done it by makin' a page for me without my askin'. From the moment I first logged in to it, a few weeks after she'd made it, I was immediately put off by all of the old familiar faces that had popped up asking to be my "friend." All the drug addicts, criminals, sluts, lowlifes and vagabonds of yesteryear flooded my screen and tangled my nerves like a bad acid flashback. The online high-school reunion had begun. When I'd shown

Helen how many of my old friends had found me on there, she became jealous.

"I haven't had any of my old high-school friends find me on here," she'd admitted spitefully. I remember thinking *Well, that's probably because they remember you*. I then changed my password so she couldn't spy on me, which she woulda.

I ignored any friend requests that didn't have personal messages added. That saved me a lot of time and really narrowed down the list. This was good because I actually had no interest in talkin' to most people, and I didn't want to dog-paddle through the memory swamp when I'd wasted so much time and rent checks cleansin' myself from my dark past in the Sunshine State — cleansin' with cheap white lightnin' and fistfuls of trazadone and lamotrigine. If I was expected to bother with people in any capacity, I figured they'd better start things off with some sort of openin' letter like decent people used to do.

Most of 'em didn't. But Whitney did.

It had been nothin' at first. I was with Helen, and I don't mess around behind my woman's back, not even when she's a moody bitch who seemed to feed off of startin' petty fights. Whitney was just a gal I'd gone to high school with. We'd never dated or made out on a crate behind the Jiffy Mart or nothin'. I never took her in the back of my El Camino, like I did with all those young cowgirls, back in the dust of the badlands where we'd all drag-raced 'n' bonfire-boxed away our poverty-stricken youths.

Whitney's emails were basic at first, just playin' catch-up on the last 16 years.

She was married with three kids. She seemed to love the kids but was bored by her husband. Really bored. She loved country music — both the old stuff, like me, and the new stuff, like everybody else. She'd never left our hometown. She didn't work, but she was trying to start some sort of outlaw-chicks calendar shoot. I could see why, from the photo shoots she did and posted on her web page with allurin' pride.

She had a solid body and a lustful, feline face. Her hair was a tornado of dyed flame — gets me every time — and she had very nice, although very fake, breasts. The outlaw flare was obvious. In the photos she was always smokin' and brandishin' semi-automatic weapons. Sometimes she'd be runnin' her tongue up the barrel of a magnum. Sometimes she'd be firing them topless. In one picture, she actually had a shotgun in her hands that was shootin' milk all over the place. Not sure how she did that one. Soon enough she was sendin' me private ones that were much raunchier — full nudes and full autos.

It's a Florida thang.

She wore raggedy jean skirts that were cut so short you could see her panties, and she must have had a treasure chest full of cowboy hats because she always had on a different one. Her ears were riddled with earrin's that hung about her shoulders in festoons, remindin' me of my boyhood hero, Mr. T, but somehow arousin'. Her lipstick was always slightly smeared, like she'd just been kissed, and her hair and clothin' was always rustled, like she'd just been rollin' in the hay with a grizzly.

Whitney, the redneck wet dream.

We had emailed back and forth a little, but then when I broke things off with Helen I made the mistake of lettin' Whitney know. Her messages became heavy flirts that I would have responded to if I hadn't been so despondent over Mama's ailin' health and my breakin' up with Helen — yet another failure in an ever-growin' line. But just a few nights before my flight to be with Mom, in a moment of drunkenness, I emailed Whitney my phone number, which she'd been askin' for. Now she was reachin' out to me, practically *beggin'* for it, and I needed a distraction from reality. I needed a euphoric painkiller, even if for only a few hours, and the Lortabs the doc had given me for my old prison rodeo injuries just weren't cuttin' it. The mind can be so cruel and relentless with heartache. Sometimes sex is the only thing strong enough to really distract a man from real sufferin'. I'd always tried to remind myself that my obsession with it wasn't as bad as a lot of other addictions and sins. Man is a carnal bein', after all.

I figured dumbass Ron must have told Whitney I was in town, or that maybe my phone "checked me in" to Florida without me knowin' it. Helen had certainly set up enough weird and unnecessary applications on the darned thang. At any rate, Whitney knew I was here, and I knew she was makin' her intentions as clear as the fountain that spews in front of that damn hospital.

But she was married. Unhappily, but married.

Jesus, is this what you'd call a mixed blessin'? Or is this my old friend Lucifer, who doesn't ever need the Internet or a cellphone to find me? He finds me just fine, and too often at that.

I looked at myself in the rearview mirror.

"Shit, it's good to be home," I said, "but it's a bad day for the angel on our shoulder."

* * * * *

Whitney didn't want to be called, only texted.

Her text: *Discretion, please.*

Her next text: *I will call you soon from another phone.*

I ate my sub while sittin' in yet another parkin' lot, watching' the afternoon clouds move over that flat land, rumblin'. It was hot, but it was better that I stay in the car anyhow. I avoid public places as much as I can these days. People rub me the wrong way, and I rub them even worse — like sandpaper. I deal with 'em enough as it is at the meat counter, and it's the worst part of my job.

My phone rang.

"Yeah?" I said, hopin' for Whitney.

"Mr. O'Rourke?" an older woman said back.

"Who's callin'?"

"This is Nurse Cooper at the hospital."

"And?"

"I just wanted to let you know that your mom is going to be resting for a while longer now."

"Y'all make sure she gets water, now."

"She's asleep now."

"Every time I see her, her lips are all dry and cracked."

She gave me a pause and an exhausted sigh — the nerve of this old witch.

"Sir, we are giving her the best care we can right now, okay?"

The tone seemed condescendin'.

"Naw, she's dyin'," I said, "and you're milkin' her like a tipped cow."

Another pause.

"You can speak to my supervisor if that pleases you, sir."

"Hell, I can speak to anyone I want," I said. "Just don't go havin' the bedside manner of an eel."

She hung up on me. Folks often do. It was a landline, too, so it had that satisfyin' slam sound.

I tried to go back to my sandwich but I just wasn't hungry anymore. Now I was gettin' the rage heat that likes to burst inside my chest like a dynamited mine.

Not now, Lord. I asked for a heart attack, but not now.

But it was just the anger — the heavy and very physical reaction I have to rage. The nurse practitioner I see for my meds tells me it's some kind of "explosive" disorder mixed with PTSD, brought on by years of underground boxing, my prison time for manslaughter, and havin' grown up with a father who thought he was still back in the jungle, killin' Charlie, when I was a little boy.

I reckon that's why Pop pulled us all outta Texas 'n' moved us to Florida in the first place. It was a familiar jungle — just like the one he'd suffered in during the bloody, frenzied dreams that would make him shoot up in the middle of the night and grab his young son, having him lock and load because he thought the gooks were behind the tree line.

Florida. It was hell and home all at once.

The phone rang again, and I wanted it to be the hospital then, maybe a supervisor I could give a solid tongue-lashin' to.

"Yeah?" I asked.

"Billy Joe?" a younger woman asked. No one had called me that since I'd passed 30, except for Mama a'course. And this wasn't Mama. Dad and Sis being dead, I didn't hear people call me Billy Joe much. Up north it was just Bill. In prison it was William Joseph O'Rourke, just like at my baptism. Only someone from the bad old days would call me that.

"Speakin'," I said.

"It's Whitney, baby."

Her voice turned sultry. She was givin' me her best Jessica Rabbit. It was workin' too. The burnin' in my chest turned into a stirrin' in my loins.

"What's your 20, girl? Where ya' at?" I asked.

"Somewhere discreet."

"In Melbourne?"

"Holopaw. But we can't meet there."

"Let's meet soon. You want discretion. That's understandable. But I'm on a tight schedule."

She didn't know why I was in town, or so I guessed, and I didn't want to bring it up. I was about to ask how she heard I was in town 't all but she made me lose the thought with her retort.

"Really? A tight schedule? Well, I have something even tighter for you, cowboy."

I looked at myself in the mirror again for no real reason.

"Tonight?" I asked.

"I have a place picked out. How is Christmas for you?"

"Kinda crass for a holiday, but the town of Christmas ain't too far from here, I reckon. About fitty miles as the crow flies."

"Only takes me about 40 minutes on my bike."

"Still ridin' that old rice burner?" I asked, remembering her winning races in the badlands long ago.

"Oh, no, no. It's only hogs for this gal."

"Nice upgrade. Glad you're still a rider. Good to see that some things never change, Whitney."

"Call me Scarlet Red."

I chuckled at how thick she was spoonin' out the fantasy.

"Do you want me tonight or not?" she said back, insulted.

"Alright," I said, tryin' to laugh it off. "Scarlet Red it is. That's cool. It suits you."

"It's discreet."

There was a pause. The only one speakin' was the angel on my shoulder, tryin' to get me to back out. But Scarlet Red interrupted.

"I like the pictures on your page," she said. "You don't have too many up, but you still look great. Still a boxer, huh?"

"No, but I try to stay in shape."

"Good. Me too."

"I can tell."

There was another weird pause.

"So where's this place we're going, 'n' when?" I asked, that devil on my shoulder doin' cartwheels and frothin' like a rabid hound.

"Can't wait to get down to it, huh?"

"I could use a good lay."

"Likewise, and I remember when Sally Slader fucked you in the back of your El Camino one night. Remember her?"

"Mightin' if I saw her again. I'm better with faces than names."

"She sure remembers you. She said you were the best fuck of her life."

I snorted at that one.

"Come on, shush. We were just teens, her life at that time was pretty short. She must have been 16 at the oldest."

"Those were the days," she said, oddly pausing. "So, anyway, there's an old motel out on Possum Lane. It's called The Palm Tree Inn. Be there in about 'n hour. I'll take care of the room. Tell the clerk you are there to see Scarlet Red and he'll give you a key. He won't ask you who you are, and you shouldn't offer it none. Discretion, above all else, please."

"All right then."

"I'll arrive shortly after and will go right to your room. Don't wait for me in the lobby — it's shitty anyway. I'll come to you, understand?"

"Yeah. Can I bring anythin'?"

"Nope. I have everything we need, plus some fun surprises. I'll be bringing some Natty Ice for myself, and as I recall, you're a whiskey drinker. I have a bag with everything we need."

"You make this sound like a drug deal," I said.

There was a pause.

"Listen," she said. "I have outfits you're going to enjoy. Plus, I just had my implants replaced a few months back to make them bigger. You can do whatever you want to me as long as you can keep your trap shut about it."

I took a deep breath and the rain began to sprinkle the windshield.

"It's rainin'," I said.

"It rains every afternoon in Florida, remember?"

"I mean it might delay me a bit. But I'll be there, and I'll tick a lock. Discretion's only fair."

"I'll give you enough time," she said. "I'll see you soon, cowboy. I'm gonna fucking *breathe* you."

She hung up.

I looked around the parkin' lot as a string of loose carts drifted in the wind of the oncomin' storm.

She'd gotten me turned on — a welcome distraction.

* * * * *

The motel was more like a river shack, although it wasn't near anythin' but a canal filled with redneck rubbish: a hubcap, part of a washin' machine, some floatin' cans of Icehouse and plenty of cigarette butts.

I'd driven up the state roads through the showers. I preferred 'em to 95 because you could ride 'longside the beach 'n' rivers instead of just seein' concrete 'n' cattle. The stink was just as bad either way, so I figured I might as well get a nicer view for as long as I could.

I was glad we were meetin' in the town of Christmas.
It got me outta Melbourne for a while and gave me
somethin' new to look at, even if it wasn't any prettier. I
was also glad that Whitney didn't expect me to drive to
Holopaw. It was closer, but it was a bad place, much like
what Melbourne was when I was growin' up there, when it
was dirt roads 'n' fruit stands and people shot up stores in
fits of mania. Holopaw had recently made news because it
was the home of a group called the American Front, a
buncha Nazi-skinhead assholes who the FBI's Joint
Terrorism Task Force investigated for tryin' to start some
kind of half-assed race war — serious Charles Manson shit.

Better to be in Christmas and accept my shameful
early present from Santa there — my busty new toy
wrapped in lingerie and nipple rings.

I walked in and a fat man in overalls looked at me
with one eye as the other wandered in his skull like a lost
rat. He didn't say nothin', just stared and chewed his
Redman. Maybe that's why he couldn't speak, I thought.

"I'm here for Scarlet Red," I said.

He spat into a mason jar that was half-full of his
personal swill. He turned around and grabbed a key off of a
corkboard and placed it on the counter.

"You're in 13," he said.

I reached for my wallet — *Mama raised a gentleman.*

"Already paid for, sir," the fat man said.

The lamp flickered even though the storm was over.

"You go back outside and take a right," he said.
"You're the last one on the left. Very private."

"Yeah. *Discreet,*" I said and nodded, lookin' at the
floor to avoid his evil eye.

He knew, and I knew he knew — and fat, redneck piece of spittin' shit or not, I felt ashamed in front of him, much like I imagine a man must feel being caught by a cop posin' as a hooker.

"You enjoy your stay, sir."

As I turned around to walk out, I noticed the velvet paintin' on the wall near the door. It was of an 18-wheeler rollin' smoothly down the highway with a Dixie flag burned into its grille. Above it, hoverin' like the Holy Ghost he is, was our savior. The artist's depiction was strikin'. But this was not the sufferin', dark Christ of my pseudo-Catholic upbringin'. This was the softer, happier Jesus, offerin' warmth and guidance, like Saint Christopher would have before he done got disbarred or whatever.

Below the paintin' was a wooden sign that was engraved with a phrase: Happy trails to you. Y'all come back now, ya' hear?

* * * * *

There was an old TV on a dresser in front of the queen-size bed. The room was small, but big enough for what we intended to do. It had a clean toilet and a stand-in shower. No tub. The lamp by the bedside had a shade that was cracked, but the room looked clean, too. The linens smelled of fabric softener, which reminded me of Mom.

I thought of her when she was still nice and plump, before the disease had withered her, hangin' the big stuff out to dry on the line in the backyard of the house the bank took from us when Dad had died. I thought about how when she hung those sheets out there, she'd sing Billy Joe

Shaver songs — her favorite country star, and the man she named me after. She always said she liked to sing for Rebel, our first dog, who was buried out there near the fence. At least he lived to be 13, unlike my poor sister.

Thirteen. That was the room I was in.

The angel on my shoulder got louder, tellin' me all signs pointed to *no*. To shut him up, I turned on the television. It was mostly garbage. Always is, and that was why I didn't have cable myself. Eventually I settled on one of those movie channels and waited to see if somethin' decent came on. It was an older movie channel that you don't pay extra for, so it had commercials. I watched an ad for a cheap tool that helped remove dents from cars. Then some Western flick came on, but I was too scatterbrained to enjoy it like I normally would.

I got a piss out of the way and then looked into the mirror in the bathroom. I hadn't shaved since yesterday and my eyes were dark from lack of sleep. I tended to sweat a lot, so I took off my shirt and jeans and gave myself a quick whore's bath with the sink and the fresh soaps.

I redressed and then sat on the bed, staring at actors playin' wild men trippin' horses and shootin' the life outta Indians. I figured almost everyone on the screen I was lookin' at must actually be dead by now. When the knock at the door came, I left the TV on as light, but I muted the sound. I said nothin' and looked through the peephole. It was dark out by now, but the glow from the bug zappers revealed her, reflectin' off of her red hair.

Forgive me, Father, for I am bout to sin like the motherfucker I am.

I let my lover in.

* * * * *

She was on top of me, backward — just how I like it. Reverse cowgirl. Her silicone breasts heaved as she breathed heavier and heavier, and the heels of her alligator boots dug into my sides, givin' me a little pain with my pleasure, which I never mind. When the deed was done 'n' she'd finished shudderin', she rolled over and just lay there for a moment, knees bent, nude except for the garter belt and boots. The light of the TV made her body piercings shine like lil' diamonds.

A diamond bullet, straight into my forehead, Colonel Kurtz was sayin' on the TV's repeated ad for *Apocalypse Now*, a movie that always made me bitterly think of Dad. I wondered then, randomly, how many women the old man had bedded in sleazy rooms like the one I was in now, before meetin' a straight-up gal like Mama to set him as right as anyone could get the man. I recalled then how I had once asked him somethin' about his homecomin'.

"Hey Pop," I'd said as we'd sat on the porch, drinkin' PBR with Rebel curled around my feet. I reckon I was about 14 by then. "When you came back from 'Nam, what was the first thing you wanted to do now that you were back in the good old U.S.A.?"

He'd taken a long pull on his cigar and replied: "I just wanted to fuck a round-eye for a change."

Whitney rolled over, and I wondered how she could possibly not be gettin' enough attention from her hubby. You'd have to be some kinda fag not to be going after a piece like that, 'specially if you had it tethered at home. I wondered if the poor sap Whitney had at home knew just how bored she was with him. But thinkin' about that made me remember how bad I should be feelin', so I just shut that outta my skull and slid to the edge of the mattress.

"Something wrong, baby?" she asked.

I got off the bed, and so did she. She got on her knees and began to stroke me while she drank the Jack Daniel's straight from the bottle.

"I have business attire I can put on if you want," she said. "Same stuff we ladies wear to church on Sunday: skin-tight dresses that cover the chest, but you put on high heels so your ass pops. Gotta make sure that even Jesus would want to take you to bed."

"Jesus befriended the whores as well as the cripples," I told her.

"I know. He loves us all. Even dirty boys and girls like us."

Before I knew it, I was on top of her again, and after a time I felt all of my feelin's of stress and anxiety and fear and hatred and despair all surge through my muscles in a vascular wave, burnin' into one single discharge that I was about to fire into the body of this woman I barely knew. She never broke motion when it hit. My legs shook and I rolled off of her. She ran her hands 'long my legs and rested her head in my lap, kissin' on it and such, gigglin' like a little girl who'd just farted in class.

I fell backward, happily exhausted, relief warmly mistin' me like powder in a barbershop. Whitney excused herself to the bathroom, and so I stared at the television, watchin' Lee Van Cleef ride off into the sunset.

* * * * *

I was handcuffed when I awoke.

She stood over me in a red vinyl corset that could barely contain her implants. She was all in crimson: thigh-high boots, gloves, and a choke collar, all matchin'. I didn't like the cuffs, but I liked what I saw.

"Scarlet Red," I said and smiled.

My smile faded when she revealed the pistol from behind her back. It was a silenced Glock. From the look of it, I figured it held about 10 to 13 .45 auto rounds per magazine.

"This ain't a game I enjoy, girl," I said. I made sure my voice was hard and firm. This was *not* sexy to me. Might be fine for some of those perverts and kinky types she was tryin' to sell them pinups to, but that kinda violent threat don't fly with a man like me.

"What's wrong? Big cowboy scared of guns?"

"They just ain't toys, and certainly not sex toys."

"Not for some."

"I'm serious, now, Whitney, I don't like this …"

She smacked me across the face, hard.

"The name is Scarlet Red!"

"Take these cuffs off of me right now," I said.

She ran the barrel of the silencer across my cheek.

"What is the point of all this?" I asked.

She got down on her knees and straddled me. She wore no panties. She began to glide back and forth, making me feel like I was under a swingin' guillotine. There was no trust here, and where there is no trust I revert to my animal instincts. When you've gone to prison, or even just when you've been a fighter, that never leaves you.

"Can you feel it?" she asked.

"What?"

"You're getting kind of hard again, despite the fear."

"Of course I am, it's a physical reaction."

She took me in her hand, and then we were havin' sex again. She ran the Glock up and down my ribcage gently. That's when I said somethin' I never thought I would ever say to a woman.

"Stop fuckin' me!"

She just giggled like a kid again and kept ridin'.

"I'm gonna bring you to the edge," she said. "Don't you understand? Don't you get it yet?"

I struggled against the cuffs. I could tell they were cheap.

"Sex. Murder. Art," she said, matter-of-factly. "You're a religious boy. You know what a succubus is, don't ya?"

I grit my teeth, refusing to feed her sick delusions.

"Well," she said, "in case all that boxing has made you punchy, I'll tell you: A succubus is a female demon that drains the souls of men with sex."

"You're out of your gourd, girl," I told her, pullin' at the cuffs. "You're human, you lunatic!"

She noticed me tryin' to break outta them and she sneered, slippin' her free hand behin' her back. She pulled out a medieval-lookin' dagger that's handle was designed to look like some kinda demon's face with bat wings.

Oh bury me not, on the lone prairie.

She was too quick and totally on target. The blade penetrated me where the shoulder meets the chest. It was all muscle, though, at least. She hadn't penetrated nothin' important.

"I'm gonna take your soul tonight," Scarlet said, ridin' me harder now. "The others I got off of web pages. Sex Date and Ashley and all those hookup sites. They were mostly lonely, pathetic men. No one even seemed to miss them much once they were gone. I wanted someone big and strong — a no-bullshit cowboy, like the old days. I want a good kill to be proud of."

I tried to shake her off of me, and she slowly slid the dagger across my belly, just enough to make me bleed. She ran her fingers into the wound and then brought them to her mouth, lappin' at my blood like a goddamned, starvin' pooch.

She looked at me then, smilin' with my blood on her teeth. I went to move again, and she put the barrel of the gun in my face, tryin' to force it into my mouth. I turned my head away.

I'll be with you soon, Pop and little sis, provided the good Lord'll let me walk those streets of glory after all I've done.

"I remember when I heard about you going to jail," she said. "That scumbag raped your little sister and you hunted him down and pummeled him like the coward he was. You're a real man, and you're going to make for one fine trophy."

"Just another notch on your bedpost 'n' Glock?" I asked with a snarl. "Well let me tell you somethin' …"

I thrust, feelin' our pelvic bones pound harshly. I wanted it to hurt, and I felt her tighten as her body began to shake.

"I shouldn't have killed that som'bitch that raped her," I said in a fury, tears brewin' in my eyes. "It was the biggest mistake of my life. In killin' him, I lost years to prison. My sister felt nothin' but guilt 'n' shame, and she done killed herself. I wasn't 'round to stop that. It broke my parents' hearts — tainted us as kin forever."

She knelt over me now and leaned on the headboard so not to lose her balance, but still she held the gun in one hand and the dagger in t'other. She seemed to be in ecstasy, the sick bitch.

"When you climax," Scarlet said in a moan, "I'm going to kill you at the exact same time. Then I will breathe in your dyin' breath, and eat your soul."

"You listen to me, you psychopath," I replied, "ain't no grave can hold my body down."

She slipped the blade up under my ribs, piercin' my flesh once again. She wasn't strong enough to drive it through bone, but I was strong enough to snap those cheap handcuffs apart.

With my hands freed and my wrists bloody, I took a wild swing and punched her in the face with everythin' I had. I felt that pretty jaw give way and she flew backward, tumblin' across the tussled sheets and hittin' the floor with a thud. I felt a tooth juttin' out of my fist. The gun went off with a blip, hittin' the television and messin' it up in a way that filled the room with loud, blindin' static.

I pounced like the animal I know I'd reverted to.

Her face was a mess — a second tooth was blood-splatter-stuck against her cheek. She drunkenly tried to raise the gun, and I stomped down on her arm, hard, like it was a cockroach. The gun went off again, the bullet vanishin' off somewhere safely away. I yanked the pistol outta her hand and pointed it at her as she wiggled out from under me.

But that wasn't going to be enough for the likes of Scarlet Red.

What I saw on that floor was another wild animal. Whitney wasn't there 't'all. There was only Scarlet Red: a self-declared demon. And she wouldn't goddamn stop.

She lunged at me with the dagger, and for the first time both the angel and the devil on my shoulders sang in unison. I fired, shootin' her right in the face. A hot spray exited the back of her little skull, and then her body crumpled like a discarded doll in an attic.

She lay there, dead by my hand.

Someone's wife and mother.

I ran to the bathroom, vomited, and began to wash up.

* * * * *

Once I was cleaned up and dressed, I looked 'round the motel room. Panic was settin' in and makin' me all scatterbrained. No 'mount of pills 'r booze could fix it now. The fear 'n' pain was all too fresh. But I had to be careful with details, now more'n ever. I poured whiskey on my wounds. Then I made a sort of bandage usin' the bath towel and one of Whitney's leggin's as a rope to tighten it to my bleedin' chest. I dressed and then used a smaller towel to wipe down everythin' I thought I'd touched. I then pulled all the sheets off of the bed, 'n' the pillowcases too — anythin' with my DNA. I rolled it up into a ball, usin' another leggin' as a tightenin' rope to hold the ball together.

I stepped over to the front door and cracked it just such.

It was late and the lot was empty.

I saw the Malibu, an old Ford, a beaten Hyundai and Whitney's Harley. It was a long hog, immaculate, and all white.

And I saw and behold, a white horse, and she that rode thereon had a dagger and a Glock; and there was a mask given to her, and she went forth conquering, until now.

I walked to the Malibu with the dirty linens and put them in the trunk. I pulled out my phone to look up a number, but then walked to the payphone to make the call. I had to call someone from the bad old days. A number I had hoped to never have to call upon — one that I could not call from a number that could be linked to me. I recognized his voice, even though it had been a lot of years. It filled my mind with flashbacks of our time in those cells or liftin' weights in the yard.

"It's Bill," I said.

The line was silent for a moment before he spoke again.

"Hello, Bill. What's the situation?"

"Remember that favor you owe me, Duane?"

"Every day that I'm breathin'. I know that's why you're callin'. That's why I got right to the point now, and I repeat: What's the situation?"

"A cleanup."

"I'm on a secure line, are you?"

"A payphone."

"What's the cleanup, and where?"

"A woman."

"A woman? You? Seriously?"

"She gave me no options. No other way out."

"She a hooker?"

I thought about that.

"I'm not really sure anymore," I said.

"What the fuck is that s'posed to mean? Get clear, man."

"Okay, she's not a hooker. She's just some woman. Things went bad."

"Sounds like it, shit."

"I'm in Christmas."

"You shittin' me?"

"No," I said. "I'm in room 13 at this hole called The Palm Tree Inn."

"Yeah, yeah, I know the place."

I paused, shock settlin' in.

"Really? It's a shit shack in the middle of nowhere."

"Exactly. That's why it's a hot spot, man, shit. I've been there myself and I'm tellin' you, brother, you're in a *bad* place alone. You need to get out of there *now* and make sure no one sees you. Lock the motel door. Leave the woman. It won't take us too long to get there."

His strong voice was reassurin'. I found it hard to believe that it was *I* who had saved *him* from gettin' that shank in the yard all those years ago. Duane was so much tougher than me. Maybe that's why he stayed in crime when he got out and I went into the butcher shop. Only now I'd butchered some crazed housewife from Holopaw, and my hands were shakin' for the first time since I was a child.

I went back to the room and grabbed the whiskey bottle. I washed and wiped down the Glock and the dagger too. I was tempted to take them, but I knew Duane would be more professional with disposin' of the murder weapon than I would. Plus, it was her gun anyway. I doused her in whisky a bit — where I'd been inside of her. I then splashed where we'd been on the bed too. I went to her bag and took all of her cash, hopin' it might look like a robbery or somethin' in case someone came in before Duane's boys could. I saw her cellphone and grabbed it too, thinkin' of the texts. I was relieved to see it was one of those disposable, untraceable ones. A burner, as the dealers call 'em. I took it anyways and threw it in the river on the drive back to Melbourne.

* * * * *

I slept in a chair in the hospital but didn't ask them to treat me or even hint that I'd been cut up. I'd stopped at an all-night drugstore and then bandaged myself on up by my own self. I reckon I was doing all right, and I'd already had painkillers on me anyway. No need for no doctor to be snoopin' into my business.

I was waitin' to hear that Mom was awake. I wanted to see her 'n' hold her again whiles I still could. I knew she wasn't long for this here world. That's what I was down there for in the first place, and I do believe that's why God punished me for leavin' her side even for a little while. I truly do.

It was around 7 in the mornin' when my phone rang and woke me. It was an unlisted number. A man I did not know told me the cleanup was done, and then he hung up right away, leavin' my paranoid questions in the hands of my faith in Duane.

I walked over to the nurse's counter.

It was fat-ass Nurse Cooper behind the desk.

I showed her no kindness, and stared at her like a mean cat, puttin' those murderous eyes o' mine to use.

"She up yet?" I asked.

"No, but she will be soon, for breakfast. And before you ask, she has had plenty of water, and some Chapstick too."

"Good."

I stood there for a moment, my thought patterns derailed.

"Is there anythin' I can get her?" I asked.

"Sir, all she's been asking for is you."

I bit my lip to hold back the tears just as my phone began to ring again. I didn't excuse myself but instead turned away rudely and walked outside, out into the all-too-warm day.

It was Helen, and this time I picked up.

"My God, Bill, are you all right?" she asked when I answered.

She was in one of her better moods, I could tell. But after what'd happened, she didn't seem so crazy after all.

"I'm fine, honey bee."

She laughed warmly.

"You haven't called me that in a while," she said, and it was true. I wasn't sure how to feel about that.

"Listen, I can't talk long, Mom's going to be awake soon. What's up?"

She sighed.

"You're going to think I'm crazy," she said. "Like you always do."

"Not this time."

There was a long silence where she just breathed sweetly into the receiver. I could almost smell the sweet mist of the perfume she wore and sold at the beauty counter in that department store across from the butcher shop.

She confessed, "I dreamt that you died last night."

My heart sank, and a chill went across my flesh at the same time.

"How'd I go?"

She began to get choked up, and sniffed back a tear.

"I don't know, you know how dreams are. We were in the woods and it was snowing, like that last time we were out hiking in Vermont. The leaves were all gone from the trees, and the branches seemed to reach down for you like they were alive and furious. They became like knives or claws, trying to rip you apart. But you fought them off and then ran away. That's when I started chasing you. I was calling out your name in the dark but couldn't find you."

She got choked up again and had to stop for a second.

"Then I heard this clanking sound. I turned and saw you hacking away at all the dead trees with an axe, killing them, protecting yourself but also protecting me. It made me feel so afraid for you, and yet I felt so safe."

I stood there, starin' blind at the fountain. I listened to her breathe into the phone like a ghost, the same breath that had whispered so many small nothin's into my ear when she was tangled in my embrace.

"So, then," I said, "how'd I up and go?"

She took a while to answer.

"You killed all of the trees and then collapsed. I fell down beside you and you were clutching your chest like you were having a heart attack. I tried to pound on you, to resuscitate you, but your chest began to pool with blood. But when I tried to give you mouth-to-mouth you just kissed me, sweetly, like you do when we make love. I pulled away and looked at you. You were smiling. You told me to calm down and that everything would be all right."

She paused again, and a black bird flew down and perched before me on the fountain, pickin' at the bread some old biddy'd been throwin' down there.

"Well then," I asked her, "was everythin' all right?"

"No, Bill," she said. "You died right there in front of me, surrounded by all of those dead branches."

There was a long silence between us that was heavier than an anvil. I just stood there lookin' at the fountain, through it, absorbin' 't'all.

"Helen," I told her, "I'm okay. I'm safe. Plus, it's springtime now in New England. Soon there'll be leaves."

"Are you saying there's hope?"

"Always, just in different ways."

"I miss you so much, Bill."

"I know you do, honey bee."

"Will you come back to me?"

"Look, I want you to get some help, Helen. Pills, a therapist, or perhaps even God — I don't rightly know, but you need somethin' to help you find balance. I know that's a lot of judgment comin' from a beaten-down redneck like me, but you need to hear it."

"I know. But you're not a redneck," she said. "You're so different from all the other men I've been with, all Northerners like me. I guess that's why we argue sometimes. A cultural thing. But I don't think I could go back after being with a Southern gentlemen like you, Bill. You're no redneck, you're an honest-to-goodness cowboy."

I thought that I didn't know what I was and doubted I ever would.

"Well, let's not argue that," I said. "What's important is that you need some sort of help."

"I can accept that. But who's going to help *you*, Bill?" she asked. "You've been through so much, and the God you turn to just keeps dumping more upon you! Is it God who is finally going to help you?"

"He already has."

She sighed, and there was a quiver in her voice.

"I don't understand," she admitted.

"I have been blessed."

"Oh, for Pete's sake, you're the one who's talking crazy now. Listen, when you come back," she said, "I want you to come to me, not God or booze or anything else. Come to me. My arms are open and so is my heart. They always were, Bill. I knew I loved you the moment you touched my hand."

I took a deep breath. She could always talk real pretty when she wanted to.

"I'm sorry, honey. But this is the final scene."

She paused before speakin' again.

"What are you telling me?" she asked.

"I'm tellin' you that the cowboy has to ride into the sunset."

She began to sob, and I walked over to the fountain. She started sayin' somethin' else but I dropped the cellphone into the water, destroyin' it forever. The splash frightened the black bird and it took flight, screechin' away, leavin' me alone out there with all that goddamned sun.

Behind me, Nurse Cooper had come outside.

"Your mother is ready to see you now, sir."

* * * * *

I walked into the dimly lit room. It was filled with stale air that smelled of medicine and blood. My mother was a shrunken skeleton of herself, whacked out on morphine to the point of delirium, and there were hoses runnin' all in and out of her like she was some morbid puppet. Her hair, which had once been so long, blond, and beautiful, was now reduced to grey tufts from the treatment.

I knelt beside her and noticed she had the brown scapular around her neck along with her usual St. Jude. I looked at the image upon it, of the blessed Mother cradlin' the infant Savior, and of the image of two hearts pierced by one dagger.

I love thee o most precious, sacred and immaculate hearts. Please, guide me.

I reached down and touched my mother's hand. I wrapped mine 'round hers, just as I must've done with her finger as a wee baby. She awoke, and she smiled at me, her lips lookin' better but her face sunken and sallow with the disease. Her fake teeth were still in her jar, soakin', so her smile was the horrible grimace of the dyin'. A trickle of bloody water ran out of one nostril like a pink tear, and her eyes watered at the very sight of me.

"Sonny boy," she said, "my lil' Billy Joe."

She was the most beautiful woman in the whole world.

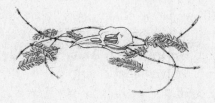

Video Express

The town itself seemed right out of a super-8 horror film, and that excited Steve all the more. The unkempt state road had brought him through the center of Wickham, and its remains were like that of so many small towns since the recession. Hollowed-out shopping plazas and abandoned homes sat rotting where the heart of the suburb used to be, sulking like a cemetery of the American dream. But Steve was a hardcore horror nerd, and he couldn't help but associate the desolation with zombie apocalypse scenarios and memories of a million cookie-cutter backwoods slasher flicks, the very sort of movies that had him driving out to Wickham in the first place.

The ad had popped up on *Horrorzone*, one of the blogs he frequented the most. It covered all aspects of horror entertainment, from rare film scores to collectible action figures. He'd found a lot of genre gems through links the blog had posted, and so he had high hopes for this one — high enough to make him drive across state lines to find the place. The ad had been a single banner, nothing fancy. It read *Video Express* and had a drawing of a locomotive with a VHS tape reel as wheels. When he'd clicked on it, he was brought to a bare-bones website that promoted an old, family-owned video store. The photos of the place, while few, revealed rows upon rows of video boxes, many still in the giant clamshells from the '80s. Posters and cardboard cutouts were displayed like a shrine to a lost age of home entertainment, easily sparking Steve's strong sense of nostalgia. The information on the page was incredibly brief. It just advertised the address and boasted *Classic videos, hard-to-find collectibles, VHS and Beta*! It puzzled him, knowing that even big chain video stores were dying in this computer age of direct downloads and DVDs by mail. He thought that perhaps it was going out of business and cleaning out the inventory, or that it was a novelty place for self-proclaimed movie geeks like himself, but the website gave no indication of that. It seemed to just be a video store, but perhaps that was the gag. With only an address to go off of, there was only one way to find out, and it seemed like a fun way to waste a Saturday.

He slowed down as he hit the next intersection, hoping the GPS would regain a signal, but the blue triangle just floated aimlessly on the screen. *Piece of crap*, he thought, reaching for the directions he'd printed out as backup. He read them over and eased the Hyundai forward, paying closer attention as he exited the state road and wound through the neighborhood. As he crept farther into Wickham, the potholes grew deeper and more frequent, and the cracks in the gravel sprouted taller weeds. The houses passed by his windows in moldy, broken blurs. He realized he hadn't seen another car in a while.

"What a ghost town," he muttered, straining to read the street signs through their rust and grime. "It's like *Children of the Corn* out here."

He made a few wrong turns before ending up where he needed to be, which was Aurora Road. He followed it to the New Haven Plaza, a dilapidated strip mall with a huge marquee for long-gone shops, laundromats and diners.

Steve wondered if any of these places were in business at all, but upon turning into the parking lot, he could see the bright-red neon of the letters reading *Video Express*, drilled into the concrete above the little store. The *Open* sign glowed pinkly in the window near a poster for the old Stallone movie *Cobra*, which was framed in white bulbs that flickered in a circular pattern, as if to shout, "Now playing!"

Steve felt his inner fanboy starting to somersault. He rapped his fingers on the steering wheel as the excitement boiled. He parked and stood in front of the place, marveling at the acute detail. He felt like he had traveled there in a time machine. The place had the same feel as the little video stores he'd frequented as a kid. He fondly remembered going with his dad and brother on weekends to such shops, back when the novelty of watching movies in your home hadn't yet worn off. He'd wandered the shelves, hypnotized by the hand-drawn cover art of the rental boxes, enticed by their promises of explosive action, big breasts, and fantastic monsters from beyond. His dad would always get something with a muscle-bound man out for revenge, his brother would pick out some sword-and-sorcery tripe, and he would select a ghastly terror that they would roll their eyes at him for. Killer dolls, masked maniacs, midget monsters, bloody power tools, and psychics in homes that dripped protoplasm. Even as a child he had reveled in the genre. Now, as an adult, he not only loved it, but also felt a strange sense of sentimentality about it. Collecting the very movies he had rented as a kid, and better yet, the ones he had always wanted to rent but never got to, gave him the same feeling of warm joy that most people get from going home to Nana's for Christmas. But if collecting the videos was nostalgic fun, standing there in front of Video Express was truly a nostalgia orgasm.

Next to the *Cobra* poster were some handmade signs that were taped to the glass.

Membership deposit of only $30!

We also rent VCRs!

Weekday Special: Rent two videos, get one free!

Make every night a ride on the Video Express!

Steve opened the door, smiling wider when he heard the brass bell ringing above him. It was tied to the door on a shoestring: completely old-school. He was greeted by a life-size cutout of Freddy Krueger grinning, with his arms crossed, next to a giant bin filled with former rentals that were now for sale.

"The budget bin!" he said to himself, delighting at the memories as they came flooding back in an awesome tsunami.

The store was small but filled with rows upon rows of wooden shelves that housed pyramids of video boxes. They were all video cassettes. No DVDs or Blu-rays. He noticed that they all had numbered clothespins on them, and he had a flashback to how that used to work: The videos themselves were always in the storage room. If the display box had a pin on it, that meant the video was in. The customer would take the pin to the counter, and the owner would go and get it, finding it based on the number system. He'd forgotten all about that until he saw it here. From the look of things, this place really was renting the videos. He couldn't understand how they stayed in business, but he loved it. It had more horror-nerd appeal than a hundred conventions.

There was a counter at the other end of the store. Behind it were a few VCRs stacked side by side. They were all the old-fashioned metal kind, heavy as lawnmowers and almost as big. One of them hummed so loudly that he could hear it across the store, and it had an eerie blue light emanating from its video slot. As he walked toward it, he passed a few televisions that were suspended from the ceiling. They were all playing trailers for decades-old movies. A small line of static tracking danced along the bottom edge of each screen. Next to one of the sets was an inflatable toilet with a goblin coming out of it, a promotional piece for the film *Ghoulies II*.

"Dude!" Steve said aloud, pumping a fist with happiness. "This place is the soapy tits!"

"Can I help you find anything?" a voice asked from behind the counter.

Steve looked back and saw a man standing there now. He was in his 40s, with a mound of blow-dried hair. He looked oddly familiar, too.

"I was just admiring the inflatable ghoulie," Steve said.

"Yeah," the man said, "yet another *Gremlins* ripoff. When is the little-monster phase gonna go?"

"I love those, dude. *Critters* and *Troll*. Hell, even *Munchies*. Classic!"

The man seemed puzzled by this.

"Okay," he said and shrugged.

Steve was surprised that he wasn't more enthusiastic.

"Are you the owner?"

"My family owns the place, yeah."

"My name's Steve. I drove down to check the place out. It's very cool."

Steve began to walk toward the counter, and as he did so there was a sudden blur in his vision. There was a gray flicker, like television static flashing in the air. He blinked hard, and it was gone.

"Hi, Steve," the man said. "My name's Charlie. Are you a member?"

Steve looked closer at Charlie, still trying to place him. He had strong features and hard eyes that gave a stare worthy of a Western.

"No, I'm not a member. At least not yet."

"Well," Charlie said, still stoic, "it's a $30 deposit."

"You really rent videos here, man?"

Charlie squinted, annoyed by the question.

"Come on, man, what the hell does it look like I rent? Furniture?"

That's when it dawned on him: the evil sensei from *The Karate Kid*. Not Mr. Miyagi, but the bad guy's coach. That's who Charlie reminded him of. He was an absolute dead ringer.

"Well," Steve said, "you just don't see too many mom-and-pop video stores anymore."

Charlie shook his head slightly and reached under the counter. Steve half expected him to come back up with a baseball bat, but instead he brought out a massive binder. He took out a sheet and handed it to him, along with a pencil. It read *Membership Form* at the top.

"Just fill this out," Charlie told him.

"Well, I'm really interested in buying some movies. Are the ones in the bin over there the only ones for sale?"

"Yeah. The other ones are full price. About $70 each."

"Seventy bucks? Seriously?"

"That's the current rate for new VHS tapes, man."

"Oh," he chuckled. "I remember that, back when they were crazy expensive. Man, you're really committed."

Charlie leaned on the counter. He had a look on his face that warned that he wasn't sure if he was being insulted or not.

"What the hell does that mean?"

"Nothing, man," Steve said. "I'm just going to check out the bin."

He backed away, wanting to avoid any confrontation. The place was cool, but Charlie's service didn't exactly thrill him. Was this supposed to be some sort of interactive theater? The guy was playing up the family-owned video store circa 1985 with strange ferocity. It was a little much.

He delved into the budget bin, sifting through the clamshells. He passed by the cornball comedies and summer-camp movies. He bypassed a few sports bloopers, crime capers and ninja sequels. There were a lot of golden turds in this pile, and they were all cheap, many of them long out of print and forgotten. He fished out a few for himself, thrilled to have found such rare cult flicks as *Things*, *Monster Dog*, *The Burning Moon*, *Sledgehammer* and *Rock N' Roll Nightmare*. All of them were in their original packaging, too. He popped open *Monster Dog*'s clamshell to see if these were just re-creations, but they were authentic. These were official releases and former rentals, complete with the *Be Kind, Rewind* stickers on the cassettes.

"Score," he said to himself.

He brought the videos up to the counter, but Charlie was gone. He figured he'd returned to the back room. It was just as well, because Steve still wanted to browse, and it was easier without Charlie hulking there. He put the tapes down and looked at the VCR that had been humming. The blue light came from inside of it, which didn't make much sense to him. As he looked at it, the light pulsed within, as if something was sparking or igniting. A bit of azure mist began to seep from the cartridge flap. He thought it was an electrical fire, so he went to call for Charlie, but as soon as he opened his mouth, another dizzy spell came over him. That strange static filled the air again, and this time he could hear it: the loud, nagging white noise of a dead screen. He leaned on the counter and held his head, shaking away the buzzing. He opened his eyes again, and the static dissipated.

"What the hell was that?" he asked himself.

He looked around, wondering if there was some kind of projector that had created the illusion. He figured it had to be part of the gimmick of the place, like a little added bonus in 3-D. But if it was, he couldn't figure out how it was being done. He walked through the aisles and over to the wall, searching for a light machine or some other trick device. There was nothing. But in the far back he came to a small closet door. It was locked. A sliver of blue light came from the slit at its bottom.

"Did you need help finding anything, hon?" a woman asked from behind him.

Steve turned around and came face to face with Linnea Quigley, his favorite scream queen. He'd know her anywhere, having seen *Return of the Living Dead* so many times, as well as many of her other movies. He even owned a bootleg of her horror workout. It was the actress, he was certain, and yet it couldn't be her. If it were, she would have aged at least a few decades. This Linnea was exactly as she looked in *Night of the Demons*, and that movie was over 20 years old. He stood there, too thunderstruck to reply.

"Are you a member?" she asked.

"Um, no."

"Well, then, you should get signed up."

She walked over to the counter, and he followed her like a lost puppy, mesmerized. She was absolutely gorgeous in her tight black mini and studded top. Her curves were prominent, and her breasts had an enticing bounce — what he always liked to call the *Quigley Jiggly*. Her blond hair was frizzed and wild in that dated metalhead-chick look, with the front teased high in a hair-sprayed puff. *Damn, she looked like Quigley.*

They reached the counter and she handed him the same form Charlie had. He began filling it out without reading it, unable to keep his eyes off her long enough to do so. He was more than happy to sign up now. He would have put his hand in a meat grinder if she'd asked him to.

"We've got the best selection in Wickham," she told him. "Dad likes to keep the customers happy with all the freshest titles. Big releases and small ones; action, horror, comedies, romances — we've got them all."

He couldn't resist.

"Did anyone ever tell you that you look like Linnea Quigley?"

She smiled, and he felt his loins stir just from that.

"I don't think so. Who's that?"

"She was a movie star. I'm sure you have some of her films here."

"Was she like Kathleen Turner? She's my favorite."

"Well, kind of. Not really."

He chuckled and, politely, so did she. He signed the membership agreement and then reached for his wallet.

"These are yours?" she asked, pointing at the videos he'd left there.

"Oh, yes."

She started to ring it all up on the ancient register, and a new type of static flashed across his field of vision. It was a single line of static this time. It bounced before his eyes, crackling as it climbed up and down. Behind Linnea's doppelganger, the VCR began to billow with mist that glowed like a blacklight, enveloping her in the neon fog. He looked back at her and saw her entire body flickering, making her disappear and reappear as the sound of dead air grew louder inside his skull. Dizziness spun him around, and he braced himself on the counter. The lights suddenly went out in the store, the only illumination coming from the gray afternoon outside. He could see that the store was empty now and in ruin. The shelves and all of their tapes were gone, as were the posters, cutouts and bins. It was an empty, gutted slot in a plaza now, with cracked windows and a filthy, torn carpet. He watched the line of tracking static grow fatter in the air, widening to fill the scope of his vision. When it smoothed out, the store was intact again: lights on, shelves full, back in business.

He steadied himself, wondering if he was having an acid flashback like no other.

"That will be $42.50," she said.

"Are you doing that?" he asked. "The lights and the fuzz?"

"It's just the tracking. It adjusts the video image."

"Video image? No, I mean …"

There was a slow creaking of hinges, and he turned to see the closet door in the back creeping open. The azure light knifed out, bathing the store in a silvery sheen of atmospheric electricity. Looking back at her, Steve watched Linnea flicker again, changing her frame in an optical smear of gray. She mutated into Charlie in a sudden blip, as if someone had simply changed the channel on his reality. Steve now felt his bowels beginning to churn. He tried to back up a step and stumbled over his own feet, dropping him on his oversized ass. Charlie laughed at him through a haze of cyclonic static. In quick flickers, he changed back into Linnea. His face and body began to strobe, and with each pulsation he became another video-star actor: the detective from *Death Wish 3*, one of *The Barbarian Brothers*, Fred Williamson, Shannon Tweed and Dorf. He moved through the counter like fluid, his head a hellish myriad of familiar faces. One second he was Gary Busey, the next he was Adrienne Barbeau, all between flickers of furious fuzz.

"Dad was good to his customers," Charlie said, leaning in close. "He was good to this town. But they all deserted him when the big chain video store came. Goddamned *Big Star Video*. They were huge. They had room for a hundred copies of each new movie. He couldn't compete with that. But oh, how he tried."

Steve tried to scoot back, but was paralyzed by his fear. The mist coiled around him, the smoke serpentine and seductive. The whole store flashed.

"Dad put the family into serious debt trying to keep this store alive," Charlie went on. "By the time he finally did go out of business, he was on a second mortgage. As if that wasn't enough, he'd grown sick. Pancreatic cancer. That's what the doctors said wasted him away. But I know it was a broken heart."

Once again the store flickered with gray static, and he saw it again as it truly was: a dim, abandoned place. He noticed that one old and rusted VCR was still on the counter, long forgotten. It whirred in overdrive, pouring out the strange mist that generated it all. But Charlie had lost his illusion too, and that redirected Steve's attention. Charlie stood before him asa maggot-riddled husk, his decomposed flesh like blackened alligator hide. His bottom jaw was missing, and he had two hollow pits for eyes, both of them churning with feeding insects.

Steve screamed and started inching backward in clumsy scoots.

"Do you know what it does to a teenage boy to watch his father disintegrate like that?" Charlie asked. "All he ever wanted was a little shop to provide for his family and to entertain the neighborhood. All of his members deserted him for Big Star. It was despicable. He died broke and ashamed, all because his customers had no loyalty, no respect for a family business."

The flickering brought the store back to life, full of boxes and vintage charm, and Charlie was Linnea Quigley again. She leaned in close, teeth bared in a snarl of bloodlust.

"I didn't just want revenge. I fucking needed it."

The VCRs behind the counter turned on in unison, the word *Play* glowing like butane flames on each faceplate. The closet door flung all the way open now, and even on the floor Steve could see the silhouettes emerging from the blinding haze. They shuffled along slowly, their feet dragging and their arms limp at their sides. The televisions came alive too, not playing movie trailers this time, but rather showing what Steve deduced to be clips from Charlie's life, like a presentation to coincide with his story.

"It was just a simple fire to begin with. I wanted Big Star reduced to ash. I didn't intend for the fire to spread, but I wasn't exactly sorry that it did. I was just a first-time arsonist. I didn't know any better. That's how I ended up trapped in there."

Steve looked up at the set, watching a young Charlie dousing Big Star in lighter fluid and cackling in the glow of the smoldering store until part of a display toppled over and pinned him. Steve turned away as he saw the teenager begin to burn alive.

"At least I took a lot of the traitors with me," Charlie said. "The entire block went up in smoke that night."

Charlie snickered as he told his morbid tale. Behind him, the shapes had lined up, swaying side by side as if stranded at sea. Some of them were charred to the point of barely looking human. Their husks were encrusted in layers of tenebrous, cracked flesh. Others, however, were ethereal-looking, adrift in the blue light, one with it. The fog grew denser.

"Look, man," Steve said, struggling to get to his feet. "I've got nothing to do with all of that. I'm not even from around here."

"No one is from around here anymore. Wickham is long gone. Damn, don't you ever just wish life came with a rewind button so you could go back to simpler, happier days? This town was my family's home; now it's just a wasteland. But I still need new members to keep Dad's dream alive. Every video store always needs new memberships, and new souls give me the power to rewind."

Charlie extended his arms as if presenting the store to him for the first time. Everything pulsed in the spotlight, the clamshells snapping like traps and the cutouts stretching taut in the azure static. Steve realized that the illusion of the video store was exactly that: a rewind on space and time, all orchestrated by this mad poltergeist.

"This was Dad's dream," Charlie said. "I vowed to honor it, even in this hellish beyond."

The other members of the store began to close in on Steve, engulfing him. Their rotted fingers tore at his flesh, dragging him toward the smoldering closet from whence they'd spilled. He tried to twist in their grip, but it only caused their nails to sink deeper into him. He tried to scream, but the only sound that escaped his throat was of television static, a deafening, nightmarish fuzz.

"We're so glad you chose to join us, Steve," Charlie said, leaning forward with a laminated membership card. "Thanks for making every night a ride on the Video Express."

Giving From the Bottom

With the electricity cut off, the only light in my bedroom came from my neighbor's obnoxious holiday decorations that burned candy-colored piss radiance from dusk till dawn. I sat on the scuffed-up hardwood floor, my back against the wall, my knees pulled to my chest for warmth.

They'd turned the gas off, too: Merry Christmas, Lewis.

I was on my last bottle of rye whiskey, relying on the constriction of my blood vessels to numb me to the stab of the cold. I had plenty of cigarettes, nothing to eat, and a huge pile of cardboard boxes filled with my ex's shit. I sat there staring at it with a combination of longing and annoyance, taking long pulls from the bottle.

I'd been sober for nine months. Then she walked out and took my willpower with her. Now I was on the floor in our broken home, unemployed, wishing for a drunkenness that would not come. I was back from my break, back into the raw sewage of my solitude, back in the bottomless bottom. Meanwhile, she was out there, with him, probably in a luxury hotel room in some warm climate, a martini glass in one hand and his crotch in the other. All the random crap she didn't need yet was here with me, sealed up in water boxes from the grocery store, sitting in the corner like a monument to all of my many failures.

The cell phone rang. They hadn't cut my service yet. So I clicked it on.

"Yeah," I said.

"Hey, Bubba," Sal replied.

We hadn't talked in months, but that was just how it went with us. There were three basic reasons he called me: nostalgia, despair, and need. Otherwise he was usually adrift, and I had, up until recently, been busy being good.

"Hey there, Sal, how's my cousin doin'?"

"I'm doin', I'm doin'."

He sounded a little wired, but not totally coked-up, which I was grateful for. There was a slight tick in his voice, but the whiskey was slowing me down now too.

"When did you get out?" I asked.

"Six weeks ago."

"How's that working out for you?"

"It's OK. I'm staying with Jeanne."

"I thought she dumped you."

"So did I. Turns out she's not as smart as she looks."

He laughed and I didn't. Then we fell silent for a moment. From the noise in the background, I assumed he was driving.

"How about you, Bubba?" he asked. "You still sober?"

"Sure," I said and took another pull from the bottle. I decided not to ask about him.

"I can't believe it's Christmas Eve already," he said.

"Another year gone."

"It goes too fast."

"And faster every year."

"Amen to that, Bubba."

We fell silent again for a moment, and then he said, "Listen," which let me know that he needed something from me.

"Listen, if you're looking for work, I've got an easy job lined up. I heard about Adrian leaving you and about you getting shit-canned from your gig. You know you can always count on me, right?"

"Right," I said, even though it wasn't really true. It was important for Sal to think that he could be there for people who were always there for him. But all they could count on him for was disappointment.

"Lewis, man, you should've called on me," he added.

"Just wanted to be alone, I guess."

"Its not good for you. You should be getting out there and starting over. Go party. Get a woman. Get some dash in your pocket."

"What's this job you've got lined up?" I asked, knowing it was something I shouldn't do, something that could further demolish the straight-line life I'd worked so hard to create for myself.

"It's a total baby dance, Bubba. No worries, easy turnaround."

"When?"

"Tonight."

Things can fall apart so fast in life. I couldn't believe I was considering this already, but what else was there? I told him to head on over, and hung up. Then I finished off the last of the whiskey in one long pull and threw the bottle against the wall. It shattered, and the glass fell like tiny, discarded diamonds across the cardboard boxes that just sat there silently, like cheap coffins sharing pieces of my butchered heart.

* * * * *

"Do we have to listen to this godawful shit?" I asked.

Sal had Christmas music jingling out of the stereo in Jeanne's Ford Probe. The cheer and merriment of its rancid, childlike, singsong crap was making my bowels churn.

"Dude, it's Christmas Eve," he said. "What the hell do you expect the radio to play?"

"What's wrong with Black Sabbath?"

"Come on. Where's your holiday spirit?"

"I deposited it into your mother's ass. Now turn it off."

He did, and the sound of the winter wind filled the night like an omnipotent poltergeist. I popped open one of the beers from the six-pack at my feet.

"For Christ's sake," I said. "That 'Santa Baby' song is bad enough without it being some guy singing it."

"You're mean as a whip tonight, Bubba."

"Then find someone else to do this for you."

"It's not for me, man, it's for us. In the long run, you can make some good money off this little job. Just you wait and see."

I didn't reply, but just looked out the window at the tree lot on our left. It was nearly empty, and only sad-looking undesirables remained. They bent from the weight of the freshly fallen snow, making them look limp and pathetic. I gazed ahead, and darkness and ice cloaked the road, giving it a beautiful drabness: the true face of December.

"You never liked Christmas much, huh, Lewis?"

I shrugged. Sal went on.

"Even when we were kids, you never seemed to get too excited."

"There was never much to get excited about."

Sal knew what my youth was like. He'd grown up in the same house. I couldn't believe he would say something so asinine.

"Is that why you hate Christmas? Because we never really got one?"

"Sal, if I hate Christmas, it's because I hate being lied to, and Christmas is a lie that everyone agrees to tell."

That shut him up for a few minutes. But silence, much like sobriety, is something Sal never could tolerate. He couldn't shut up any better than he could stop cheating on his girlfriend. A lot of his chattiness was a result of his decades of substance abuse, his blood so toxic that it was always using his brain like a boxer uses a speed bag.

"Say," he said, "you remember that one Christmas when we had that bonfire party out by Madison Creek? I was about 17, so you must have been about 15."

"Holy shit. I had forgotten all about that."

I couldn't help but smile at the resurrected memory.

"It was amazing that we had the turnout we did, it being Christmas and all."

"Our friends were all like us," I said. "They wanted to be anywhere but home for the holidays."

"Yeah, like Joe Ziati and Frank Millan."

"Total burnouts."

"They were there. So was Lynne, and her sister, too. We got so fucking wasted that night. All that Mad Dog, speed and weed. Not to mention the ecstasy everyone was into back then. I think Danny was there, even, with Alicia."

"Jenny Johnson was there, too," I said. Mentioning her made Sal grow suddenly quiet. He loved to reminisce more than anyone else I knew, but he never liked to talk about the dead. If someone were in jail or rehab or just plain out of their mind with misery, he would talk about them without a tear, but when you mentioned people who had gone the way of all flesh, he became more uncomfortable than hemp underwear.

"Yeah," he said, finally. "Jenny was there, too. With you."

It was a sore spot. We had both had our affairs with Jenny, but I had been with her first and last. Sal had dated her for only a few weeks, and she did it more to get back at me than anything else, though Sal would never see that. But either way, she was dead, and Sal didn't like to think about death. I, however, was very in touch with it, and thought of my dead friends and family often, especially around the end of every year like this. But even I didn't talk about Jenny much. It wasn't just that she'd died that made it so hard, but how she'd died: as a crack fiend digging through her carpet, smoking anything that looked like it might be a morsel of a rock.

As we drove on through the blue-moon night, I tried to think of her, rosy-cheeked before the roaring bonfire that Christmas so long ago, her hands staying warm in my coat pocket while we smoked a joint together, me holding it up to her chapped lips. Jenny was one of those sweet girls I'd held on to so tightly because they could never be that sweet again.

Sal pulled his woman's car into the empty lot behind the green of the country club and shut off the lights. He found the darkest corner, under a withered tree limb with heavy shadow, and parked.

"You sure this is a good spot?" I asked, cautious.

"Well, we can't park at the plaza."

"No shit, MacGyver, but there might be some kind of security guard farting around in a little cart or something, just itching to prove himself."

"Don't worry, Bubba. I've been scoping this deal out for a while. I know the area. You remember Tina, the little bubble-assed spitfire I was nailing all summer?"

With Sal there was always an endless stream of faceless sluts trailing his yesterdays. I didn't bother keeping track of them. Most I never even met because it all ended quicker than it began.

"Not really," I admitted. "I think you mentioned her once. Was she the stripper with the missing finger?"

"No, that was Mya, a beautiful but worthless bitch. Tina was the one who hooked me up with all the free samples before she got shit-canned for her sticky fingers. She worked at the damn place. That's how I know it's such an easy hit, Bubba."

He slapped my shoulder and smiled a yellow grimace, proud of himself. His mouth was blistered, dry, likely from crystal meth; the twitch in his eyes suggested it.

"Listen," he said, "we zip through this part of the golf course and come out into the back of the barbershop. It'll be easy to get in there. It's an old place, run by old men. No fancy alarm system. No night watchman. No video camera."

"But we have to lug the tools there and back, on top of the swag. If someone sees us out here on this course, were done."

"That ain't gonna happen, Bubba. It's Christmas Eve. Everybody is deep in eggnog. This is the best possible time. We're gonna load up on this one. It'll be smooth sailing till the Fourth of July."

I thought it was sad how full of shit Sal was, and insulting that he thought I'd be stupid enough to believe his exaggerations. But it was even sadder that he lied so much that even he started to believe his own nonsense a lot of the time. Still, I had already agreed to do this, so there was no real sense in holding a grudge about it. After all, I hadn't fought it when he had pulled into my driveway earlier that night.

I got out of the car, and Sal popped the trunk. I reached in and grabbed the small duffel bag. It was the same one he'd had since high school, with the faded Iron Maiden and Led Zeppelin patches on it. The bag clinked and clanked like weights in a gym. I slung it over my shoulder and then reached in with both hands for the sledgehammer.

"I don't fucking believe this," I said to myself, astounded by what it had come to, and so quickly. A total snowball effect: losing the job, then Adrian leaving, then the booze, and then this. I was back to this again, the hellish bottom, the stinking corpse's butt crack of my life.

Sal locked up the car and smiled at me again like a rotting jack-o-lantern in the moonlight. He was already getting antsy. I wondered briefly when was the last time he'd slept.

"You got that all right?" he asked.

"I'll manage."

"I appreciate your help with the sledgehammer."

"It's why I'm here."

"I just can't swing that thing with my shoulder the way it is."

Sal was always in pain, and it was always somebody else's fault. Sometimes I thought he just used pain as an excuse to get high — he certainly used it as an excuse whenever he was in a clinic or doctor's office. But his shoulder situation was legitimate. He'd had trouble with it ever since he'd run his car into the telephone pole on his fourth DUI. So I carried the hammer, and the tools, and didn't really mind once we got moving.

Sal turned and started walking, and I followed him through the soft snow. The night was clearing now, and everything fell under an eerie winter blue-black. For a while, the only sound was our boots crunching and the occasional jangle of the duffle bag swinging.

"Through here," he said when we reached the rear parking lot of the small shopping center. There were no streetlamps in the rear, and only one security light at the far end. The place was almost asking for it. I followed him to a door in the brick wall, and he pointed at the lock that I had already been looking at.

"So simple, Bubba. It's got just a minimum throw at best, and a fragile little strike-plate attachment to the frame itself. They might as well lock up the joint with a paper clip and a wad of gum."

I dropped the bag, and we dug in with both hands. Our rhythm wasn't off after all this time, and it amazed me how fluidly we moved with the mini-crowbar and drills. In less than a minute the back door swung wide open for us, and we stepped into the odors of hair tonic and that neon scissor wash. We moved through the dark storage room, and I knocked into the push broom and stepped in a dustpan full of hair. Then we made it out into the center of the shop, which was lit by a single dim lamp over the cash register. The till jutted out in empty defiance. The blinds over the enormous front windows were not all the way down, so Sal quickly corrected that.

Sal started probing the wall behind the giant barber chairs, looking for an area that would provide adequate space but also would have a minimal amount of electrical wires. He found it near the last sink. He tore away a VFW calendar, moved an end table that was overflowing with hunting magazines, and kicked the wall with the tip of his cowboy boot. It gave pretty easily. He thumped away with the side of his foot now, finding the studs. There was plenty of room.

"Looks like the right spot," he said. "I'm gonna see if there's anything worth taking in here while you work on the wall. You want a nice set of pocket combs or something?"

"Steal me an old-fashioned straight razor so I can slit my wrists come Valentine's Day."

He snickered and wandered off. I swung back with the sledgehammer and then clobbered my way into the wall, obliterating it one slug at a time. My muscles hardened and my neck tensed as I pounded away, while my goon cousin looted the shop for whatever trinkets and other crap he could swipe — bonus swag for our trouble. As I sent the hammer's head into the drywall again and again, I felt my anger rise along with the adrenaline rush of the robbery and the sheer physical action. I slammed it over and over, all the while seeing Adrian's tear-wet face in my mind and seeing her sad, dark eyes when she handed me the ring back. I slammed away and thought of her frail arms pushing me away when I tried to hold her. Then I made the base splinter away and thought of her soft lips on that other man.

"Easy there, badass," Sal said from behind me. "Don't knock down the whole building." He got distracted as he opened one of the drawers in the barber's desk. "Holy shit. These old hicks have some cheeba in here!"

He reached in and lifted up what appeared to be at least a quarter bag of grass. He smiled and dropped his jaw all at once. The chump looked like a child who had just found 10 lousy dollars in the street.

"Should I roll us one while you work?"

"I'm done," I replied.

He came closer and saw that I wasn't lying. I'd roughly torn a 45-by-35 hole right through to the drugstore on the other side. Looking through, we could see the immaculately vacuumed carpet and the stainless-steel wastebasket with nothing in it.

"Sweet Christ, you're strong, Lewis."

"It's why I'm here."

Sal went through the passageway first, squatting and scurrying while visions of Oxycontin danced in his head. I followed close behind him, wanting to make this a very short visit to the pharmacy. Sal seemed to have the same idea, because he flew over the counter, swinging his legs up and over like a regular Duke of Hazzard. He did seem to know the place pretty well, too, and I could imagine him and Tina lying in his waterbed after marathon sex, Sal having her go over every detail of the pharmacy's backstock while he fantasized about pulling a quick job on the place. I weakly resented the fact that Sal knew I had hit a low spot and had immediately figured out a way to benefit from it. Had he asked me to play drugstore cowboy with him just a few months prior, I would have laughed till I pissed, and then would have told him to go blow a hobo. But I had regressed into that inner darkness of mine that Sal knew so well, and he knew to strike while that darkness was pitch-black. I tried not to take it personally. Sal used everybody. Sure, I was his cousin, but that never made a difference. Junkies dick over family more than anyone else, and repeatedly. Sure, he was bullshitting me about all the money I could make selling this stuff. I wasn't going to sell anything, and we both knew it. He could sell what he didn't take or feed to his whore of the week, but that money would never come back to me.

Sal unrolled the plastic bags he'd had bunched up in his coat and started dumping huge white jars of painkillers into them. He was murmuring to himself like an Alzheimer's patient, frantically scanning the shelves.

"Take it easy, Sal," I told him calmly.

But I didn't even exist to him now. He knocked away containers in a mad search for the opiates. When he finally uncovered the methadone, he was already shaking. He popped off the cap, letting it tumble to the same floor that he now slid down to. He kicked back the small bottle, taking a quick swig of the syrup. Calm washed over his face even before the drug could take effect, making him look like the Sal I'd known so long ago, napping in a lawn chair after drawing with chalk on the sidewalk on a cool September afternoon. It wasn't a smile that fell upon him; Sal's conniving grin would have cheapened the look. It was peace, even if for just that moment while the methadone began its work.

I knew then that my cousin would never get any better. All the therapy, jail time, and rehab had failed to make so much as a dent in his determination to destroy himself, to eviscerate his sanity on the rusty blade of narcotics-induced madness. I couldn't give him safety from himself. I couldn't even muster up the nerve to judge him. All I could do for him was understand.

I walked over to him and put my hand on his head, and he looked up at me with glassy, exhausted eyes.

"Merry Christmas, Sal," I said.

Then I started bagging up the rest of the methadone.

* * * * *

When Sal dropped me off back at home, it was Christmas morning, but daylight hadn't snapped on yet. The dawn was creeping up, giving just a slight pink blister to the horizon. He'd invited me to come back to his house and spend the holiday with him and Jeanne, but I told him I just wanted to crash. Had he known I had no heat or power, he wouldn't have driven off. That's why I didn't tell him.

I walked across my broken-gravel driveway and pulled up the garage door. The basement area inside was cold and drab, with deep pockets of blackness. Some of Adrian's other miscellaneous boxes were down here, waiting for the day she could be bothered to come over to my broken-down dump and gather her things. I shouldered some of them out of my way as I moved toward the stairs. I stepped up only one, sighed deeply, and then decided to just stay put.

I'd taken only one container of weak painkillers from the swag we'd gathered. I'd told Sal that it was all I wanted and that he could keep the rest. He accepted this after some forced resistance that was purely for show, and then he'd repeatedly told me he'd be bringing me money from the sales. Now I took the bottle out of my pocket and popped open the cap and took two of them, washing them down with the last gulp from the last can of beer from Sal's six-pack, which we'd ripped right through. I finished the beer and threw the can into one of my old-school, metal trashcans that sat by my workbench. It made a wonderfully loud and nasty noise.

As I listened to Sal getting further and further away in the Probe, I sighed again and hoped the painkillers would kick in soon — not to take away any physical pain, but to kill that much more prominent pain, that brutal sorrow that has sat like an unwanted mongrel dog in the junkyard of my heart for so, so long.

I went over to one of the boxes of Adrian's clothes and opened it up. I pulled out the first thing in the pile, a green sweater I'd bought her for her birthday last spring. I lifted it up to my face and touched it to my unshaven cheek. It still smelled of her hair and her soft, full breasts. I breathed it in again and again, this fading aroma that no longer belonged in my lungs. I had truly loved her, and now I hated myself for it, because everything she'd done to me in the past few weeks assured me that she deserved only unwavering hatred. Most people would say it wasn't love if it wasn't meant to be. Most would. But we don't all get swept away by perfect magic at the perfect time. In fact, some people don't ever know love as anything other than the undying tenderness you feel for someone who has licked your wounds just enough to make you feel like you were more than just a forever-imploding zero.

I flung the sweater into the garbage with the crushed beer can. Then I took the box filled with her clothes and dumped the rest of it into the trash as well. I grabbed another box of hers, filled with some papers, some old magazines and, of course, some shoes. This crap topped off the old can. I jumped up and sat on my workbench and pulled one of the smokes I'd bummed from Sal out of my coat pocket. I sparked it up and smoked it very slowly, enjoying it while I pulled forward the blue milk crate beneath me with my boot heel. I found the starter fluid in there next to the huge bottle of glass cleaner. I doused the trash can's components in the starter fluid, using everything in the bottle, taking long pulls on the cig as I drenched my ex's belongings. I tossed aside the empty bottle and took a final drag, pushing the smoke out of my nostrils before flicking the butt into the trash. It seemed to spin very slowly, and I figured that the pills were starting to take effect, kicking in faster from the alcohol and my lack of food.

Soon the flames were licking upward. I thought about opening the garage door further for ventilation, but I found that I didn't want to move. I was hunched over on my bench, just looking at the growing fire, and that was just fine by me. As I stared into the licks of the wild light, I saw everything that could have been, simply disintegrating, and so I made myself think of happier times. Another Christmas came to mind, and I saw myself with my arms around Jenny Johnson, keeping her warm by a bonfire that was not unlike the one before me now. I could feel her body, not yet withered from crack, wrapped up in my embrace, and her wanting more than anything to be within it. I saw myself there, and Jenny, and sitting across from us was Sal. His hair was whipping in the wind just like that fire, pulling away from his innocent face just as innocence itself was surely pulling away from Sal. I could see him exactly as he had been, my young and unbroken cousin, his eyes dilating as he looked into the wild fire, stoned but not hooked yet.

I closed my eyes and tried very hard to hang on to the image. I wasn't surprised that I couldn't cry, but I was surprised that I wanted to so badly.

Merry Christmas, Lewis.

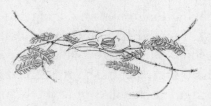

Legends

A cowboy had to ride on nights like this, when dusk cooled things and the stars peeked out of a fading sky. The smell of the horse beneath him would fuse with his own sweat, reminding him that he too was an animal roaming wildly upon but one rock in a fathomless universe. The fireflies would throb in the twilight, the owls and crickets serenading his ride in rhythm with the galloping, the sounds and sights of the prairie fusing into one lulling spell of night.

A cowboy had to ride on nights like this, just as Bronson rode now, his heels rapping the ribcage of the Tennessee Walker as it brayed, snorting hot mist. The terrain was getting rougher as they charged up the draw, but they couldn't slow down. He knew it, and so did his horse. To slow down now was suicide of the worst kind, for that ashen blackness wanted to swallow the world.

He knew why cowboys always rode into the sunset. A cowboy had to ride on nights like this, to keep his own darkness from catching him.

* * * * *

Charles Bronson died on a hot August afternoon in 2003. The pneumonia had finally taken him, at the age of 81. Even though Alzheimer's had plagued him in his later years, he was surrounded by his family in his final days, and he knew it. He went as peacefully as he could because of their love. He'd lived a long life, and while his youth had been hellish in the coal mines of Pennsylvania, his adult life had led him to be a movie-star sensation. He'd done damn well in life, and he'd been happy; just as rich in family as he'd been in the bank. He died at peace, optimistic about the afterlife and, in retrospect, perhaps a little naïve.

His moment of death was a dreamlike transition that unearthed the forgotten memory of being born. But this time, instead of leaving his mother's body, he was leaving his own. He realized in a numbing flash that all the world's artists had it wrong. Dying was like being carried by a lightning that stretched you across time, thrusting you through everything you've ever known with the backhand of a hurricane. His entire life flooded his consciousness, distracting him as he was torn from his carcass. He felt fragmented, omnipotent in his own wonderland of self-aware recollection, as if examining the very merit of his lifespan. Loves, battles, tragedies, successes, and failures, all of them as fresh as when they'd happened. He was living every memory, and even every dream, all at once. He felt like a pinball whirling through an endless machine of emotions, feeling pleasure and pain, love and fear, disgust and joy all in one explosive mélange.

He awoke as if from a nightmare, standing there in all that emptiness. It was a colorless void, infinite and without form. It gave the illusion of floating, but there was no wind.

Before he could even try to make sense of it, he heard the familiar gravelly voice behind him.

"It's one hell of a roller coaster, isn't it, Charlie?"

Bronson turned around, aware of how limber he felt. The old aches of his body were behind him now, as was his Alzheimer's. He had no trouble recognizing the man he shared this strange void with, but he was the last person Bronson would have expected to greet on the other side.

"Lee?" Bronson asked. "Lee Marvin?"

Marvin stood before him, not as the old Marvin who'd passed away, but as the younger, though still white-haired, Marvin whom he'd starred with in *The Dirty Dozen*. He stood tall in a pair of cowboy boots that matched his full Western wear, complete with gun belt and Stetson hat. Aside from being clean-shaven, he looked as Bronson remembered him from his film *Monte Walsh*.

"Nice to see you again, Charlie," he said. "It's been a while."

"I'll say it has. You've been dead for almost 20 years."

Marvin grinned his best head-shot smile.

"Only where you come from," Marvin said. "Time is not as linear as you think. But then, a lot of things are not as you think, as you're about to discover."

Marvin pointed, and Bronson followed till his gaze fell on a pinprick of light. It expanded in the nothingness to form a reflective sliver, like an oblong mirror. Bronson stared into it, stunned. His appearance was his own, but from when he was in his late 30s. He was muscular again, his body tan and vascular. His face was no longer swollen with old age. His hair was black as a crow's wing, his features as if carved from marble. It was hard to not feel a little vain.

Marvin was not the only one dressed in cowboy gear. Bronson saw that he was wearing tight jeans and a worn Wrangler jean shirt that was taut across his shoulders. A faded hat was atop his head, and the weight of the pistol in its holster made him lean to one side. He was reminded of the catalog of Westerns he'd made, from *The Magnificent Seven*, to *Red Sun*, to the fan favorite of *Once Upon a Time in the West*. He appeared now before himself, looking like a sort of hybrid of those roles.

He was glad that he still had his mustache.

"What is this?" he asked. "Are we in movie cowboy heaven?"

He was only half joking.

"Not exactly," Marvin said. "We look like this because it is how we're remembered. Our celebrity has forever burned our images in the minds of millions. Their notion of who we are and what we stood for, fictionalized or not, is what makes us what we are now. Belief is everything."

"What are we?"

"That's not an easy question to answer."

"Well, try."

"Spirits, I suppose. Angels, in a way."

Bronson let that sink in and then shook it off.

"Horseshit," Bronson said. "We look like gunslingers, not angels."

"Yeah, and this don't look like heaven." Marvin stepped closer to amplify what he was about to say. "If you're waiting for white clouds and a bunch of pantywaists with harps, you can forget it. Heaven, angels and God are not exactly what any of the religions came up with. Man, being alive, cannot know death. In many ways, even when we're dead, we don't get all of the answers."

"If this isn't heaven, then what is it?"

"A portal. Think of it as a hallway between life and death. I just came to greet you."

"Well," Bronson said and laughed. "No offense, Lee, but why you? I mean, we always got along, but you're not exactly who I would expect to greet me in the afterlife. Why not my mother? Why not Jill?"

Bronson's second wife, Jill, had died of cancer when she was only 54. Their marriage had spanned almost 30 years, and he had considered those years the very best of his life. Although he later remarried, his love for Jill had never faded, and neither had the pain of seeing her wither away, the cancer slowly eating her. He had always tried to remember her the way she had been before the cancer: young, beautiful and lustrous, riding her horses and playing with their children in the sunshine of their Vermont farm. If anyone should meet him in the afterlife, it should have been her. Instead, here stood Lee Marvin, dressed for high noon.

"I wish it was like that, Charlie," Marvin said. "I really do. There are a lot of people I would have liked to see again on this other side. Maybe we will be reunited with them at some point. But right now we've got a job to do."

The nothingness began shining in a color Bronson had never seen before. The light seemed fluid, and out of that fluid the two horses pushed forth. The horses stood next to Marvin, completing his Western theme. All he needed was a Morricone score.

"The power of belief is everything," Marvin explained. "The real heroes of the world get their 15 minutes of fame sometimes, and other times they just die on a battlefield. But movie heroes stay heroes forever. As long as there is an audience, the belief in the heroes is there. The world thinks of us as cowboy heroes, and that is what we are now, in this second level."

"Second level?"

"The next step. The second level of existence."

Marvin put a boot into a stirrup and mounted his horse. The light grew brighter, silhouetting him in a cosmic display.

"Call us angels," Marvin said. "Or call us ghosts. But what we really are is legends."

Bronson looked at the other horse. Its eyes were like two small moons glowing in the night. He waited for Marvin to say more, but he fell quiet, as if waiting for Bronson to understand. As a child of the Great Depression, toiling in the dismal mining town, Bronson had felt deep despair. In World War II, as a tail gunner in a B-29 bomber, he'd felt the adrenaline rush that came with battle, particularly when a bullet had dug its way into his arm. When Jill had died, he'd felt a shattering loss, and he knew then what it was to have a wound that would not heal. But he had never felt so confused before, so utterly lost, as he did right now. He stood there in some inexplicable phantom realm, being told he was a legend and not knowing what to make of that, not knowing where he was headed or what awaited him when he got there. There were so many questions. He figured he'd start with the simplest one.

"So, where are we riding to?" he asked.

* * * * *

They were driven as if by the wind, pulled by instinct and little else. The horses followed their rein pulls just slightly before the riders could issue them, they too moving with an unseen force, drawn like magnets to whatever was beyond the void. He rode beside Marvin, and the portal absorbed them. Bronson felt tranquil, the fluid nothingness engulfing him in a thunderous wave.

The light gave way to a more comfortable blue as they burst through Earth's stratosphere, sailing through the sky on the backs of their steeds, galloping and yet in a way flying back to the world these men had come from. The oddest thing about it was that it didn't seem odd. He was riding a horse through clouds and charging back toward the Earth below, and yet it seemed like second nature. There was no fear, no vertigo. He wasn't gasping for air, as he should have been at this altitude. He wasn't even cold.

The horses didn't break stride as they landed in the pasture. The dust was heavy there, swarming. They pulled the horses back into a trot.

"How you holding up?" Marvin asked.

"Not too bad, for having just flown on horseback."

Marvin chuckled, his gaze on the horizon.

"It's weird," Bronson said. "I feel like I know where we're supposed to go, even though I'm not sure what we're doing. I know we need to head west."

"You're right, and you'll get used to that. Follow those premonitions. That's fate guiding you."

As they carried on, Marvin began to explain.

"Since I died, I've come to figure out a few things. I don't have all the answers. All I can tell you is my take on it. The way I see it is that the afterlife, or at least this stage of it, moves in phases, much like life. You have good times and bad. Both of us had our hard years, been to war. But we also had some good times: money, fame, and beautiful women. Good and bad, like the yin and the yang and all that mystic shit."

"I never took you for the mystic type," Bronson said with a smirk.

"I never was, but we just rode horses out of the sun."

"Point taken."

"So anyway, we both started our lives off hard. We had to earn the good times in life. I think the same goes for death. We have to pay our dues before we get to see our loved ones and be at peace. I think we, more than most people, have to do this because we allowed ourselves to become heroes in the eyes of the world. We accepted those titles."

"I never considered myself a hero."

"It doesn't matter how humble you may have felt about it. What matters is how you came to be perceived. They may have just been roles to us, but they have become something more to the world."

"A news clip once referred to me as a white knight in dark times," Bronson said, remembering. "Is that what I am now? A knight in shit-kickers?"

"It is what we were becoming for all of those years without knowing it."

"Legends," Bronson repeated, looking at the small town ahead.

"Legends," Marvin replied.

"So what is it that white knights do when they come back from the other side?"

There was an ominous quiet to the town up ahead that sulked under a black plume of smoke. Bronson felt the hairs on his arm stand up, and in unison his horse became antsy. Marvin's eyes hardened, staring straight through the falling ash at the shadowy buildings ahead.

"Well, cowboy," Marvin said. "We hunt us up some demons. But first things first: I need a drink."

* * * * *

The town had seemed vacant from the outskirts, but while it was a bit of a wasteland, some stragglers still remained. The buildings were haunted-looking, with forgotten cars corroding in the relentless heat. Fires had ravaged much of the area, and smoke still lingered, hinting at more. The businesses looked as vacant as the homes, but Bronson knew, as Marvin did, that saloon keepers and undertakers never starve. They found an open bar, dismounted and tied their horses.

Marvin was as thirsty as Bronson had remembered him, kicking back the bourbon with flicks of his wrist. They'd received a few stares coming into town on horseback, but the townsfolk were few and so beaten-down-looking, as if poverty and hopelessness had long ago eaten their interest in the world around them. They didn't speak. Seeing people in such a state always reminded

Bronson of his hellish youth in the mining town, toiling in blackness.

"Another bourbon, pal?" the bartender asked. He was a heavy man in his 60s. The wrinkles of a hard life cracked his tanned and leathery face, allowing him to smile out of only one side of his mouth.

"Three fingers," Marvin said, and the barman poured.

Bronson drank his water.

"Come on, Charlie," Marvin said. "You don't have to be such a health nut anymore. The game is over."

The barman wandered off, pouring beer for some worn-out ranchers at the end of the bar. Bronson studied them, noticing their hair and clothing as well as the décor of the barroom itself. It was a farming town, he could tell, which made them stand out a little less, not being alone in wearing cowboy hats. But there was a nostalgic air to it as well.

"Something tells me this isn't the same year I left from," Bronson said.

"You're catching on," Marvin replied.

"The shaggy hair, this wood paneling, the cars out front; I'd say we're in the mid-'70s."

"I'd say you're right. Like I told you before, time is not linear. It only seems to work that way for the living."

"What about for demons?" Bronson asked.

Marvin kicked back his drink.

"The demons love nothing more than fucking up history. Whatever is happening here *now* didn't happen in *our* '70s. They've come to try to make an alternate history. If they ruin the past enough, then they contort the future. It poisons the universe."

Bronson rubbed his temples, overwhelmed by it all.

"There's no whiskey in the beyond," Marvin told him. "That's one of the many problems with it."

He put down his glass and looked at Bronson, his stare unwavering.

"When I died," Marvin began, "I was greeted by John Wayne. The first thing he said to me was, 'Sorry, Lee, but we're all out of booze, and if ever you needed a drink, it's now.' Not long after that, we were galloping through Colorado, battling these goddamned things from the other side."

"Demons?"

"I don't know what else to call them. They all look different, and they all look worse than anything you could ever imagine: turned inside out and twisted into real horrors. You always know them, though, even when they try to pass for human. You'll find that you can sniff them out like a warden's bloodhound on a prison-break hunt. It's because we're supposed to hunt them, Charlie. It's what we do now. Evil is everywhere and rampant. I don't think it can ever be contained, but we have to try to at least keep it in check."

The barman came back to refill Marvin's tumbler. He looked at them both, recognition glowing in his tired eyes.

"Say," he said, "I wasn't gonna say nothing, but I just have to ask. Aren't you fellas in the pictures?"

"Used to be," Marvin said.

"Yeah, you're Lee Marvin, ain't ya?" he asked. "And you're Charles Bronson, right?"

Bronson nodded and smiled politely.

"I knew it," the barman said. "I've seen tons of you guys's pictures. I love Westerns. You guys are the best cowboy heroes we've got."

"Good," Marvin said. "Cause you're gonna need them."

"Need what?"

"Cowboy heroes."

The barman's face grew puzzled, more confused now than starstruck. Marvin kicked back his glass and dropped it on the counter. He spoke with a seriousness that was underscored by his hard voice.

"Listen, Mac," Marvin said, "this town and everybody in it is in grave danger. You take one look around, and you can see this place is rotting like it has a curse on it. Who knows, maybe it does, right?"

The barman straightened up.

"You're the saloon keeper in this burg," Marvin continued, "you hear all the stories. Your finger is on this town's fading pulse. So, tell me about them so Charlie and I know what we're up against."

"Who?" the barman asked, growing pale.

"The demons, Mac, the same ones who are going to rain down on y'all like Hell or worse, unless they're wrangled."

* * * * *

It was like confession.

Once the barman opened up, he just had to get every last bit of it off his chest. First the crops had started withering, he told them, and then the cattle started giving sour milk. Then the draught made the farming even harder, and led to random fires that destroyed businesses, homes, and lives. Soot filled the air, combining with the Arizona heat to create a new brand of misery. The town began to sink into poverty and despair, but things hadn't gotten all that bad yet.

Whole pastures of cattle turned up eviscerated, their guts spilled across the grass in a kaleidoscope of burnt gore. But worse than that, people went missing. What little they found of some of them made what happened in the cattle fields look merciful, the remains mutilated beyond recognition. One of the heads that had been found had a smooth, perfect hole in it, and most of the brain matter had been removed in a manner that suggested it'd been melted away. Another young man's body was found by the creek, the carcass nude and twisted like a contortionist, the face still intact but the skull inexplicably missing. They found more and more pieces of their neighbors scattered across the plains like so much roadkill, and all the while the black smoke churned in the sky and sluiced through every crevice, enveloping them in a black hell.

The barman had shaken when he'd talked with them, his eyes glossing over. Though he didn't speak of it, Bronson could tell that he'd lost someone close to him in all of this madness.

After a few more drinks, they returned to their horses and headed west, their hearts guiding them and their horses with some internal compass. The steeds carried them across dirt roads that wound through the farmland and up through winding valleys that yearned for daylight. The murk was thick, bloating, and it echoed with a dull roar. It throbbed with an evil Bronson could taste on the air. He sensed it like a familiar ache. It was an ancient awfulness, he knew, though he knew not its form or name.

"The evil has returned," Marvin said.

"I can feel it," Bronson said, and he felt a twitch of terror flush his heart. It was a deep horror, like what he'd felt when he'd had to break the doctor's news to Jill that her cancer was malignant. "I've felt this before."

"Me too," Marvin said. "In Hell's Pocket."

Marvin fell silent for a moment, observing the darkness that had drowned out the sun. He had the look of a man pained by his own mind as he stared out at the gorge.

"July of '44," Marvin explained, "the Battle of Saipan, during the assault on Mount Tapochau. I was a 20-year-old Marine, fighting the Imperial Japanese Army. We had them licked from the get-go, but they wouldn't take defeat lightly. They hid in the caves, deploying under the cover of darkness. We'd find their hiding spots in the mountain sometimes and take them out with flamethrowers, Charlie. That was how it was done. Most of my company was killed in that battle. Almost everyone who landed on the island, American or Jap, lost their lives. A machine gun severed my sciatic nerve when it shot me in my ass, and I still consider that the luckiest moment of my life, because I survived a battle that took thousands of lives."

Marvin fell silent again and the darkness swelled around the red rocks of the gorge. It was rugged terrain in this part of the valley, desertlike and alien within the farmland.

"The demons know," Marvin said. "They know the worst moments of your life, just as they know mine. Our worst memories are their weapon of choice. It can overpower you. It certainly overpowered The Duke."

"John Wayne?"

"The demons killed him on one of our missions."

"Killed his ghost? How can a ghost die?"

"Just because we've already died doesn't make us invincible."

"Well, where do we go if our ghosts are killed? To the next level of existence?"

"I don't know," Marvin admitted. "I haven't had the misfortune of finding out yet."

Marvin unhitched his rope from the latch on his belt. There was a louder rumbling now. It wasn't just the smoke above, but something below, as if the earth itself was having a seizure. Their horses stirred and Bronson filled his hand with his revolver. The silver of it shined as if it were reflecting sunlight, even though they were in the belly of those shadows. It was warm in his hand, and gentle, like a mother's touch. It felt entirely one with his body, to the point where he felt like he could discharge it with his mind.

"They know we're here," Bronson said. "They're coming, I can sense them."

Marvin nodded but didn't take his eyes off the ridge. He remained so still that the ash that had been snowing down began to pool in the brim of his Stetson. He looked like a statue, reminding Bronson of Greek mythology. *Legends*, he thought, breathing deep.

"What do we do when they get here, Lee?"

"Simple," Marvin said. "We herd them back to Hell."

Bronson cocked his hammer and ground his teeth.

That's when the horizon exploded in white flame.

* * * * *

Suddenly they were everywhere.

They were as fast as they were hideous, these things with bodies like massive, skinned dogs covered in horns. The horns gleamed out of every fold, lining up in rows to form mouths that snapped the air hungrily. Dust created even more haze at the hooves of these abominations as they thundered across the plain. They moved instinctually, for they had no eyes, writhing like injured serpents in the mist. They surged all around like biblical locusts. They moved in what looked like rapid spasms, making them hard to predict. It was a wonder the beasts could gain as much ground as they did in their clumsy twitches, but in a quick lunge one went for Bronson's leg. His pistol turned it into soup. The sound of the shot was like lightning striking his very soul, reverberating throughout his entire being. He trotted the horse backward and saw that where the demon had fallen, the ground opened in a pond of black oil that boiled about the thing's body, melting it back into the nightmare realm from which it had sprung.

The stampede began. The demons spun about the ridge in a tornado of flesh. They barked blood into the air as they charged in frenzy. Marvin lassoed one of them and kicked his heels into his horse's ribcage. The steed bolted and they dragged the beast behind them in a violent spray.

Bronson set his own horse into a gallop and began blasting as he rode, splitting a few monster skulls as he followed Marvin toward the wall of flame at the edge of the ridge. When Marvin reached the gorge, he flung his lassoed beast forward, sending it into the hellfire with a scream.

"Show yourself, you son of a bitch!" Marvin howled into the smoke.

Bronson didn't understand, but he stopped trying to. Whatever Marvin was yelling at had listened. The flames twisted upward to reveal a silhouette within: the thin shape of a man. The demons behind them were charging closer, but Bronson and Marvin waited for the shadow to emerge. They had to. It oozed forward like bubbling molasses, and Bronson felt somehow cold despite the growing fire, because the face that formed before them was one that Bronson knew. The fallow hair and sunken eyes had not changed, even if his body was now comprised of demonic sludge and mangled tallow. He remembered the gruesome headlines with crystal clarity. He had no doubt who stood before them.

This was Jeffrey Dahmer's demon.

He seemed to levitate there in the white fire. His body of oil began to pulsate with fresh veins as pieces of flesh flew around him like wasps. A red circle formed, bathing him in an orb of blood. He was a horror to behold. He swam there, within his ocean of gore and madness, a testament to all that was sick and depraved. Looking upon him, Bronson remembered what Marvin had said about the power of belief. He wondered then if people's mass fear of such serial killers could empower a demon, just as mass belief in movie heroes could empower majestic cowboys in the hereafter.

He fired off a shot, but Dahmer vaporized and then reappeared as if he was one with the darkness. Bronson sensed now that the darkness was of the Dahmer demon's own crafting, and these other demonic dogs were merely lesser abominations accompanying this master monstrosity on his return from the beyond.

Bronson felt himself moving forward, and held on as his horse went up on his front legs to kick a demon with his hind ones. The wretched thing burst upon impact. Marvin charged for Dahmer and began firing his pistol. The blasts seemed to slice the gloom like small rays of sunlight creeping through window blinds, and Bronson remembered how they had rode out of the sun, and wondered about the significance. He fired randomly then at the demons in the murk. Small beams of light lingered, trailing the path of where he had fired, and when one of the demons collided with it, they went up in flames. They fell to the earth, and the oil of their realm returned to claim them. With each one, the darkness began to give way, and now he could see the sun setting on the edge of the valley.

Bronson charged to catch up with Marvin, who was chasing Dahmer with the kind of fury only a Marine could muster. Watching him ride after that ghastly thing, his gun blazing, Bronson was glad to know Marvin was buried in Arlington. He deserved it for more reasons than the living would ever know. Marvin had died long before Dahmer's story broke. He didn't know him. But he knew demons, and he refused to tolerate them. He accepted that it was his job to destroy them, just as any good soldier would have.

When Bronson caught up with them, they'd reached a jagged part of the gorge that led downward into a rocky pit. Dahmer had fleshed out but wasn't human-looking, as they were. He was more like his minions, only bigger. His face was as it had been in life, but he had a bull's body, making him resemble a Minotaur with translucent flesh. He was covered in veins that pumped black blood. Bronson could actually see it moving through him, fueling his savagery. The demon opened his mouth to reveal a smile full of razors, and cackled at Bronson before running into the gorge.

They followed him into the pit. The horses, not of this world, fearlessly charged down the twisted terrain. A few of the demon dogs tried to follow, and tumbled to gruesome deaths. When they reached level ground, they followed Dahmer as he thundered through the chasm, the ground cracking beneath him in small earthquakes. His hoofprints seeped formaldehyde.

Bronson noticed that the blackness was thickening again.

"This is his domain," Marvin shouted. "This is where he'll be strongest."

The horses slowed to a stop.

Dahmer stood before his cave, waiting. The cave was lined with bones and rotting body parts in a morbid shrine to murder. The darkness above them rumbled and began making strange clacking sounds. It took Bronson a moment to recognize the rumbling as not thunder but the sound of bombs going off. The clacking, he realized, was machine-gun fire.

He turned to Marvin, who was nearly paralyzed now as all around him the horror of his experiences in World War II came alive. Out of the murk, the images of Japanese soldiers moved back and forth, fusing with the faces of Marvin's fallen Marine brothers. The only thing louder than the gunfire was the screams, including Marvin's.

"Fight him!" Bronson yelled, but Marvin was stunned. It was like shell shock, multiplied.

Bronson began to fire at Dahmer's demon, the beams of light singeing the beast like a branding iron. Dahmer bucked from the pain, screeching. Bronson knew he had pissed him off. He knew the demon would chase him now. He had to get him away from Marvin in order to give him time to snap out of his waking nightmare.

He charged up the embankment and Dahmer followed, sure enough. The smoke in the chasm had become so thick that there was weight to it. His horse struggled just to maintain its stride. They raced on through the valley, his heart leading him west again, where he knew the sun must be, even if he could not see it. Fireflies danced at the horse's hooves. Twilight was settling. Something told him there wasn't much time, and so he refused to look back, even as the Dahmer beast roared like a freight train in pursuit.

But the darkness grew more personal.

It didn't rain down ash now. Instead, it rained down soot.

His horse charged on, both of them praying for light.

The soot was from coal, just like what had polluted the air of his hometown of Ehrenfeld. Not that it was really a town; it had been a company fief. The workers toiled there in the mines, and their families lived in the company houses and shopped in the company stores. The coal miners were forever enslaved to the company machine. His father had hacked away at that coal for long hours throughout the years, breathing in black soot until it had eaten away his lungs. In the end, he was choking on every breath. His poor father had died when Charlie was just a child, and his closest brothers, George and Tony, had soon followed. Bronson had found himself having to help support his family at the age of 16, going to school by day and working in those mines by night. Even after graduating, there was nowhere else to turn but to those black pits, because the Great Depression was in full swing.

Behind him now, the beast howled and the darkness thickened. Coal dust began to cake his duster and his horse.

Bronson remembered being 18 years old, working double shifts in the mines, worrying about a collapse with every shudder, but worrying about supporting his family more. They were so much in hock to the company store that they could barely scrape by. He'd never in his life felt as trapped as he did down in those deep, dark mines. He would never forget chopping away at all that goddamned coal and weeping at the sheer hopelessness of his life.

The Dahmer beast changed his howls now. They had become the heartbreaking cries of Jill when the cancer had turned into agony. Bronson felt every muscle in his body flex. A scream filled his throat. Outrage fueled him now. Dahmer had pushed him right past pain and fear into war mode. He spun his horse around, sitting upright in the saddle, his chest out. Dahmer skidded to a halt, confused.

"Clearly, you don't know who you're dealing with," he told the beast.

Bronson fired, over and over again, moving the hammer back rapidly with his free hand in true gunslinger fashion. Even the cordite from his pistol glowed, splitting the darkness and thinning it out. Dahmer was jolted from the close-range shots, and his wounds erupted in black geysers. Not wasting the demon's moment of pain, Bronson lassoed him, pinning his arms to his sides.

The darkness began to clear, and he saw the last bit of sunlight on the horizon. It was a gorgeous display of golden light and pink sky. It was not just the sun, Bronson knew, it was the portal. He charged forward, letting Dahmer catch fire as the last bit of that gleaming touched him now, and letting him burn as he dragged the beast, racing onward, a cowboy hero riding off into the sunset.

* * * * *

Marvin caught up with him once the Dahmer demon had been flung into oblivion as a smoldering carcass. The horizon had swallowed him. Bronson had just turned around to head back for him when he saw him galloping out of the gorge.

"It is done," Bronson told him.

Marvin looked around at the blooming twilight and the newfound peace of the valley.

"I can tell," Marvin said. "Nice work, Charlie. Sorry I froze up back there."

"Don't be. He pulled the same mind tricks with me. He had me almost in tears at the memory of my childhood.

But then he pissed me off by using Jill's death against me. As if losing her wasn't enough, he had to taunt me with it."

Marvin grinned.

"Pushed too far," he said. "Just like in the movies."

Bronson grinned too.

"Maybe this fate isn't so crazy after all," he admitted.

"Well," Marvin said, "this moment in time is safe again. Time to head back."

"You go on without me."

Marvin stiffened in his saddle.

"What was that?"

"You heard me, Lee. I'm not going back. I've done my good deed. The universe owes me."

"Owes you what?"

Now it was Bronson's turn to stare off into the hills, lost in the corridors of his mind. Silence was an art of his, but Marvin knew where he was coming from.

"You can't go see her, Charlie," Marvin said.

"Don't try and stand in my way."

"Look …"

"No, *you* look!" Bronson interrupted. "She was the love of my life. She and the family we made together were the best part of my life. Fame and fortune meant nothing next to that. I just want to see her one more time, the way she was before the cancer tore her apart. I want to see her young and beautiful and full of life. Why is that so much to ask?"

"Because if you start to change history, you'll be transforming the future. You'll be doing exactly what the demons want."

Bronson let that sink in, but it still didn't convince him.

"I won't ruin anything."

"You could ruin your own past. You could tear the fabric of reality so easily, and ruin not just your own existence, but Jill's, too. You had a wonderful life with her. Nothing can destroy that memory except you. Don't you think I have regrets? You were a loving family man. I was a bad boy living in a man's body. I lived for good times and loose women. I wish I could turn back the clock, too, but you can't change destiny. *This* is our destiny now."

The last bit of sunlight sank away, leaving only the soft glow of fireflies and stars.

"Will I ever be reunited with her?"

Marvin wouldn't lie to him.

"I don't know," he said.

Bronson sighed and urged his horse into a trot. Marvin joined him, and they rode slowly then, side by side. The fireflies whirled about them, their glow becoming like one radiant ball of warmth, guiding them back. There was comfort in that light, even though he knew his demon-hunting quests were far from over. Before entering the portal, he took one last look back at the prairie. The sky was larger than he'd ever seen it, and each star twinkled in some sort of mysterious sign. He wondered if each of them was shuttling more cosmic heroes. A breeze blew through the valley and the night air caressed his bare neck, exactly like Jill's breath when she used to nuzzle him. He could almost smell her perfume. He looked up at those glimmering stars and remembered the words he'd had put upon his own tombstone:

Of quiet birds in circled flight, I am the soft stars that shine at night. Do not stand at my grave and cry, I am not here, I did not die.

He rode beside Marvin, the two cowboy heroes fulfilling their new destiny as death's anteroom opened up in a blinding shimmer. He rode on, into the radiant beyond, a legend.

About the Author

Kristopher Triana is an author who specializes in horror and the macabre. Influenced as a child by B-movie poster art and late-night slasher fodder, he has been writing scary stories since his youth. Now a complete fanatic when it comes to the genre, he has been published in several anthologies and magazines.

He is also a professional dog trainer, an avid weightlifter, and a bit of a cowboy.

He lives in North Carolina with his wife.